NOT

A TRIO

A TRIO

(Two Stories and a Novella)

by David Huddle

University of Notre Dame Press

Notre Dame, Indiana

Library of Congress Cataloging-in-Publication Data
Huddle, David, 1942–
Not : a trio : two stories and a novella / by David Huddle.
p.   cm.
Contents: Village tale — Wherever I am not — Not.
ISBN 0-268-03651-9 (cloth : alk. paper)
I. Title.
PS3558.U287 N6   2000
813'.54—dc21   00-055980

∞ *This book is printed on acid-free paper.*

for

ELAINE SEGAL

Acknowledgments

"Village Tale" appeared in *Colorado Review*.
"Wherever I Am Not" appeared in *64*.

Contents

Village
Tale

I have a weekly appointment, but I am not her client, and she does not bill me for this hour of her time. She comes to the waiting area to fetch me; she follows me back to her office, which is furnished like a living room used only for visitors. Once inside, I stand and wait for her to close the door behind us. Then I put my arms around her and kiss her greedily. I loosen her clothes. The carpet is thick and not uncomfortable. So accustomed are we to stifling our moans and sighs that our discipline carries over to what we say aloud to each other. We murmur and whisper, but our conversation is held back. We haven't had a good talk since we got to be lovers. Claire worries about her colleague who uses the room next door. He and his client speak at a volume that comes to us as a distant drone. We have to listen to hear it. I tell Claire that I doubt he's noticed us; he would have to ignore his client to take note of the lack of regular voices coming from Claire's office.

Some mornings, though, Claire resists me. She's ashamed. She whispers that it won't be long before she can put me out of her life. "Baby, baby," I tell her. "I know," I say. I stroke her hair. I whisper to her that it's okay for her to be ashamed of me, but she ought not to feel so bad about herself. I say that I took advantage of her, I know it, she knows it. While I'm telling her these things, I'm taking advantage of her. I'm whispering directly into her ear, which just kills her. I'm kneading the muscles in her back right between her shoulder blades, where she gets the most tense. I'm letting her feel how strong my arms are, how sure my fingers are, all the while pressing up against her enough for her to feel how glad I am to see her. Claire says I'm the most natural-born slut she's ever met. About that she's probably right. I can't be around a woman any time at all without trying out some little something on her.

Every week when I show up to wait for my hour with Claire, I figure this will be the morning she'll say, "Danny, I'm sorry, I can't see you today." It doesn't happen. First the client she sees before me leaves—it's the Burtle girl everybody in town knows hates her parents so much they pay Claire to talk her out of killing them for one more week. There's a little pause while Claire sits at her desk, typing her notes on that session into her computer—the one I set her up with. Then she comes out and looks me in the eye. Sometimes I see she's on the verge of saying it—"I'm sorry, I can't see you this morning, Danny." It would be easy. I root for her to spit it out. Instead, it's, "Come in, Danny," with a rueful smile. She lets me walk down the hall ahead of her. Just inside her office, I wait for her to close the door behind us. Sometimes, with the tip of my finger—softly, softly—I touch her hip while she sets the latch.

Then it's a matter of picking up the signals. Does she want me right then, just as fast as she can get me, or does she want me to work to bring her around? This is where most men are stumbling in the dark. Since I was fourteen I've known my way around this territory. Every woman is different, sure, but if they haven't declared you a noncandidate, there's a basic principle: they want you to take them. They want you to be so smart and strong and understanding and wise and confident and subtle and affectionate and bold and witty and stylish and ardent that they just can't resist. They're on your side, really. Surprise, they want what you want! That's the part most men don't get. They figure it's like grade school, where the opposite sex is against them. Women are the enemy. So they figure the male somehow has to defeat the female.

I never argue with Claire—or with anybody else, for that matter, because the truth is I don't have what most people would call principles or convictions. I just think what I think. I read a little bit, and of course I can't help seeing what I see. But most of what I think comes from trying to make sense out of the way I am. The way I am is, to use Claire's word, incorrigible. So in this town I'm a complete disgrace. I guess I'm a disgrace wherever I am, but here in Bennington I'm a known disgrace. There are people around here who keep better track of the women I've slept with than I do myself. I'm talked about and bad-mouthed and ridiculed and laughed at and insulted. Just because of what people say about me, there's a woman here in town who spits in my direction whenever she sees me. She doesn't know me; she's never exchanged a word with me, never seen me do anything more offensive than buy my groceries or go to the post office. But she knows she hates me. I get men who give me looks that let me know what they think of me, too, but they don't usually say anything, because I've got some size, and it's pretty evident that I stay in shape. I won't, but I look like I could hurt somebody.

Here's something I'd say to those assholes who think they know what I'm all about: no woman I ever slept with ever has anything bad to say to me when she meets me on the street. I get the cast-down eyes and the blinked-back tears and even occasionally the please, can we talk? requests. But no you bastard, you son of a bitch. No God damn yous are coming from the women who actually know me. I say bear that in mind when you're making your assessments of my character.

Like it or not, I've had to accept the fact that as long as I stay here in Bennington, my reputation is part of who I am. Claire won't see me anywhere but here in her office. She says people are probably talking anyway, but as long as I'm coming here for my hour once a week, they can at least figure it's possible that I'm her patient. "It looks like I'm trying to help you, Danny," she says, and she's got just this shadow of a wicked grin on her face. Women, I'll tell you, I've devoted my life to them, and I think they're the superior sex by a factor of at least fifty-six—but the truth of the average woman makes Genghis Khan look like a tea rose.

Claire, for instance, had a first husband who beat her and a second husband who died on her; the first husband lived on the money she made and did his best to squeeze every ounce of life out of her. Claire still got through graduate school, kept her looks and her figure, then finally got herself free of that guy. She and her new husband, before he got killed, bought an old house and fixed it up to look better than a new one. She was devastated by his death, but she still got to be the best shrink in southern Vermont. And though this isn't known to anybody but herself and me, she still has the sexual vitality of a healthy teenager. You look at Claire, you see a hundred and thirty-five pounds of mildly pretty middle-aged woman. You think, well she's nice. She's nice all right—she's lived a life that would drop most men in their tracks, and she's got all her faculties intact, so to speak. I'll tell you, I'd be proud to walk into the Iron Boots New Year's Eve Charity Soirée with that lady on my arm. I make my five-hundred-dollar donation to attend that thing because I like to dance, and I like wearing a tux. I told Claire my fantasy, the two of us in our formal clothes, walking into that party, stepping out onto the dance floor and making people's jaws drop. Ms. Absolutely Wonderful and Mr. Total Disgrace, the lovely couple—in your face, Bennington, Vermont! Claire won't do it, though. "Not a chance, Danny," she said. She claims she'll be at home by herself in bed with a bowl of microwave popcorn in her lap and the TV on and plans for turning out the light as soon as she's seen the lighted ball drop in Times Square. She makes remarks like that to tell me that I don't have to feel sorry for her.

All my life I've looked for a woman who'd be straightforward with me about sex. Somebody who wouldn't be using it to pull my chain and wouldn't be whining for more time, more attention, more conversation. Somebody who wanted the pleasures of the body and the intimacy of the moment. Finally in Claire I find her, the ideal woman, the ideal arrangement. An hour of sexual company once a week. So now how do I feel? I feel teased, I feel incomplete, I feel half satisfied. I'm wanting more time, more attention, and more conversation.

I call Claire's answering service and leave a message for her to call me when she gets a chance. Getting in touch with her like this reminds me of the old days. I'm the small-business computers guy in this part of the state, I don't need to make any more money than I do, and so I'm a one-person operation. I don't put in much more than a five-hour day. So a year ago when Claire and her associates decided to computerize themselves, Claire was leaving messages on my machine, and I was leaving messages with her service all the time. Even now, if I heard that voice on my machine—"Mr. Marlow, this is Claire McClelland. Can you please give me a call this afternoon? 838-7792. Thanks."—I expect I'd experience what they used to call a stirring of the loins. The problem is that Claire and I became lovers just about the time her new computer started working perfectly. All of a sudden she wanted no more calls going back and forth between us.

"The last thing I need in the world is for people in town to think we're doing this, Danny," she said.

"I wish it didn't embarrass you, Claire," I said. This exchange took place on the carpet of her office about 7:15 on a September morning. No one else was in the building. Six-thirty A.M. was the only time slot she had been able to find that week for me to come down to her office and teach her how to move back and forth between her word-processing program, her calendar, her calculator, her billing program, and so on. I did her a favor by showing up so early. What I knew from little things she'd told me was that since her husband's death she hadn't been sleeping more than a couple of hours a night. I could have suggested we do that tutorial at 4 A.M. and it would probably have been all right with her. She seemed relieved to have something to do at 6:30. I'm an early morning person anyway; my faculties are unnaturally sharp at that time of day. Which is probably why things happened the way they did. Claire was sitting at her desk in front of her machine; I was standing behind her telling her where to point her cursor. I became conscious of the way my voice was sounding, like I was singing her a lullaby, *Now point the arrow to the little calendar there, right there, and click it twice real quickly, that's right, now*—. All of a sudden, the mental message I received from the woman sitting in front of me was so clear I almost thought she'd spoken it aloud, *Now put your hands on my shoulders very lightly so that I don't have to notice it if I don't want to, that's right, now bend closer to my ear*—.

I shouldn't have done it, I know that. It still embarrasses me
that I listened to what I heard, because I knew Claire was newly
widowed, I knew she was hurting, knew she was just about half
crazy from loneliness, knew that her sexual response to me was no
more personal than, forgive me for saying so, opening a bedside
drawer and taking out a vibrator. I wanted not to do it almost as
much as I wanted to do it. The results were explosive. Claire will
still blush if I remind her of that first time.

What makes it worse is that I even knew some of the details of
her husband's death. He'd been hit by a car here in town in a freak
accident. A little old lady lost control of her vehicle, ran up onto
the sidewalk, and dinged him just before the brick side of Hargreaves Market got her stopped. The ambulance crew was slow to
tend to Ben McClelland, Claire's husband, because they were so
worried about the old lady whose broken nose had bloodied up
her whole face and who was scared and hollering. Ben had picked
himself up; he was calm and quiet and looked okay, but he was
bleeding internally. By the time he passed out and they got him
into an ambulance and ran him up to the hospital, he was just
gone. If he'd made more of a fuss, they might have saved him. It
was so completely screwy that everybody felt like no, that couldn't
have happened that way. But it did. Ben and Claire had been married only a couple of years, and Ben had been a real sweetheart to
her after all those years of alcoholic meanness she got from her
first husband. Of course that first husband, Jim Boscowen, is still
healthy and strutting around town like Bennington's own living
demonstration of God's lousy sense of humor.

When Claire returns my call, it's a little after five. She's polite,
but I can tell she thinks I'd better have a good reason for having
called her after she's told me she doesn't want me calling.

"Claire, I want a real appointment," I tell her.

I imagine her frowning and maybe squinting at her finger-
nails. "What for, Danny? What's the trouble?"

I let a beat or two of white noise go her way. I've thought
about this question, but I haven't made a decision about exactly
how to answer it. Finally, though, I do have to say something. "My

lover and I are not communicating," I say. "I think I might be frustrated."

Claire chuckles. For a moment I don't like it, I think she's making fun of me. Then I catch that edge in her voice; she means to be acknowledging that our arrangement has some problems. "I don't know if I can help you, Danny. I might have a conflict of interest."

I'm right back at her. "You're the only one who can help me," I say. The way it comes out of my mouth and my chest, I know it's something I've needed to tell her.

She sits with that a few moments. I do, too. Voices from far-distant conversations yammer at us over the phone wires. When she does speak up again, Claire's voice is soft. "Do you want to have a real appointment instead of the one I've already scheduled for you next week?"

This is a hard question even though I can see that it's a fair one. I concentrate on reading Claire's tone. Does she mean that if she's going to be seeing me as a client, she doesn't want to go on with our arrangement? Or does she mean that her feelings are going to be hurt if I suggest we put our arrangement on hold? And what exactly do I want? Do I want to be both fucking her and talking to her, or do I want to stop the one and start the other? "No," I say. "I want both," I say.

She clears her throat. "Both," she says in this neutral voice. I hear, or I imagine I hear, her turning the pages of her appointment book. "I already have you down for Wednesday morning at ten. I had somebody who canceled an appointment I made for Tuesday afternoon at five. How does that sound?"

I write it down. "Tuesday at five. Thanks, Claire."

I'm cheered up way beyond what the situation calls for. My whole weekend is fierce workouts, very responsible eating and drinking, worthwhile reading, some decent sports on TV. I feel calm and strong. The weather's mild for December, so that it's comfortable taking my regular three-mile run each morning. During the afternoons and evenings I'm on the phone with one lady friend and another, but we're just checking in with each other.

Nobody, including myself, seems to be all that needful, even on Saturday night, which is the hour of truth for us singles.

What I notice is that I'm doing these little tidying activities, straightening up the house, puttering around the yard. While vacuuming out my Miata, I even find myself thinking about going down to the office to start getting my tax documents in order. That's when I tell myself to back off, go easy, maintain perspective. All I'm about to do is have a normal conversation with my lover, nothing I have to change my life for.

Tuesday morning, though, is one of those days when the weather broods. The clouds are low and heavy, the air cold and wet. You know snow is coming, but there's going to be a wait before it gets here. Bennington days like this make me want to drive over to Albany to catch the first flight down to Miami. It's an old anxiety, one I never will get used to. I stay close to the office, don't take any calls, and try to lose myself in checking out a couple of new pentium laptops that Compaq has sent down. By four o'clock when I come home to catch a shower, I think I have my thoughts in order, but I'm not feeling as steady as I'd like to.

I shave close but with an old blade so that I don't cut myself. I put on a white shirt, a navy cashmere sweater, and a new pair of wool pants. I brush my hair carefully, but the shaving lotion I use is the usual stuff. Claire shouldn't be thinking that I'm making a major effort to impress her, but I would like her to be noticing my strong points. I look better at forty-two than I did at twenty-two. I've got just enough muscle to be solid, not buffed out. I carry myself well because my body feels right. My face isn't pretty, but I've been told it's got character. When I walk through a restaurant, I turn some heads. I'm not a guy who makes women drool, but I am one who makes them take a definite look and maybe say to themselves, well now.

I've never been in the waiting area of Claire's building this time of day. I don't seem to be able to relax. There's only one other person here with me, a middle-aged lady I don't know but whose face tells me she's been through some significant hell lately. It's after dark, the first snowflakes are just beginning to sift down outside, and the fluorescent light in the foyer buzzes cruelly down on this lady and me; we're sitting in a location that identifies us to any passerby as people with problems, people who need help.

The hour turns, the shift changes, one by one the four-o'clock clients gather their coats from the little closet out here and leave the building. Nobody looks anybody in the eye. Phil Chadwick, who's got an office upstairs, comes down and nods to the lady waiting there with me. She sighs heavily as she gets up to follow him back upstairs. Frank Collins, who's got the office next door to Claire, puts on his hat and gives me a curt nod before he leaves the building. Then Polly Currier, who's got the other upstairs office, comes down with her chin buried in the collar of her fur coat. Without even a glance at me, she glides out the door. I'm sitting here by myself, aware of the late-afternoon emptiness of the place and of Claire and me, in separate rooms, being the only two people left in the downstairs. It's an oddly pleasing moment. I don't mind that whatever she's doing back there is keeping her from coming to fetch me. Finally, though, I hear her door open and her footsteps coming down the hall toward me. "Come on in, Danny," she says. There's no smile. When I stand up, I'm aware that she's watching me a little more carefully than she usually does.

Claire's always radiant—or that's how she seems to me—but right now it's humming at a very low level. She's tired. In her royal blue jacket and white blouse with a ribbed front, she's got some style, but her face is puffy, and her eyes look like she's been rubbing them. Also, her hair could use some attention. I've never seen her look like this, though the thought has occurred to me that listening to people's troubles for seven or eight hours a day could be wearing.

I walk straight to the sofa and take the side where I imagine most of Claire's clients sit. There's a side table with a box of Kleenex and a small painted carving of a box turtle. I'm tempted to pick the turtle up, but I don't because I know I'd fiddle with it and show Claire just how nervous I am.

Claire settles herself in the chair nearest me. Then she stands up and angles the chair a few inches around so as to face me more directly. She sits again, folds her hands in her lap, and looks directly at me. The silence stretches. This is a quality of Claire's that I like—she can just sit with the silence in a circumstance where most people would have to start jabbering—though I've wondered if it isn't just a shrink thing, a trick to get the other person to reveal himself.

"Well, Danny," she finally says. "This is different, isn't it?"

Her expression is too complicated for me to read easily. There's the tiredness that even her face is fighting; she's very close to giving up the effort to be professional and to letting her features just sag. There's the acknowledgment that she and I have been intimate, that no matter what gets said right now, she and I have that nakedness in our past. And now that I've got my scopes focused like this, what I think I'm seeing most clearly is Defense, with a capital D. I almost blurt out, "I'm not here to hurt you, Claire," but of course I don't do that.

"Maybe different is what we need, Claire." I try to keep my face neutral. I'm taking all the shake and shimmy out of my face, my voice, and even my body.

She gives a little sideways nod.

"When I'm here with you the other way"—I give a little nod of my own down toward the carpet—"I feel like a thief. I come in here and think I'm taking something from you." Again I nod toward the floor. "Then when I leave I see I'm not taking anything with me. It's this strange feeling—like I didn't get caught, but I didn't get any goods either."

I look at her. If I can say something like this out of nowhere, what does that mean? Sometimes I wonder just exactly where my life is located. I'm living two lives at once, one I know about and another one that stays out of my sight.

"It's the same for me, Danny," Claire murmurs. "I feel that way, too." She lets some silence float on by. "But I'm not sure I want to feel any other way."

We sit with that for a while. I watch Claire carefully press her skirt against either side of the knee she's crossed over the other, then lift a hand to her hair. All of a sudden she knows that it's been some time since she brushed it. Her fingers catch little loose strands here and there, tuck them in, and smooth them back.

There is such intelligence in the movements of her hand that I wish I could take a movie of it to show to her. Her mind has moved on to other topics, but her hand continues with the grooming errand she sent it on. I'm thinking that all my life I've made too much of these unconscious gestures that women make. I'm moved by the woman who's so absorbed in something that she isn't aware of pulling on her bangs or stooping to adjust a loose sandal or jiggling a foot or hitching up a bra strap or fiddling with a bracelet. Too many times it's been something like that that got me interested in a woman.

Claire stands up and walks over to her desk in the corner of the room. "Have you seen this?" she asks. From a stack of papers she pulls a poster that I can't quite make out until she walks it closer to me. It's a red circle with a red slash through it; inside the circle is a baby in diapers sitting with its arms up and a big grin on its face, the kind of kid they use in the Michelin tire commercials. "Friend of mine sent me this," Claire says. When she sees that I've understood it, she turns and carries it back to the desk. With her back to me she says, "Another middle-aged woman without any children."

I can't read her voice, and I don't know what she means to be telling me. "You don't feel bad about that, do you?" I ask. I'm a little ashamed that I haven't wondered about why Claire never had kids with either one of her husbands.

"Of course I feel bad about it." She turns to face me but stays standing at her desk with her hands down and clasped together as if she's teaching a class. "Any grown-up who doesn't have kids would have to have some regrets. The question is, how bad do I feel about it? Some days I feel like I'm a freak of nature, like I've completely botched my life. Other days I think I'm one of the few sane people I know. What about you, Danny?"

She's caught me off guard. "I don't think about it that much," I say. This makes me feel like the dumb student in Claire's class— Uh, I don't know, Teach. I make another effort. "It just never seemed to be an issue, Claire, because I never got married."

She squints at me. "Did you ever get a girl pregnant, Danny?"

Suddenly, the conversation feels dangerous. I remind myself that this is what I wanted—real talk. "Yes," I say. I do some squinting of my own, but I keep looking directly into her eyes. "I did that."

She takes a step toward me. "What did you do about it?"

"We took care of it, Claire. Do you need the details? Is this really what you want to talk about?"

"But you thought about it then, didn't you, Danny? You thought about having your own kid? About your own kid being alive with you here in the world?"

"I thought more about being married to a girl I didn't want to marry."

Claire takes one step closer and leans forward. "All right, Danny. You say that after you've had sex with me, you feel like you're leaving empty-handed. You didn't really take anything from me. Or I didn't really give you anything you could take with you. Just what exactly is it that you think men and women give each other?"

I have to say that it's exhilarating to see Claire angry. I keep my mouth shut mostly because standing over me with her eyes blazing and her face flushed, she's such a sight. But I also need a second or two to process what she's said. Something does eventually come to me to say. I pitch it as softly as I can manage without actually whispering. "You said you felt that way, too, Claire. Like you go away from it—like you go away from us being together— empty."

Claire's anger starts to leave her, but she turns toward her chair before I can see all the expressions that come along to replace it. When she sits and arranges herself in the chair and meets my eyes again, her face is composed, but it's also sad and serious. Which I appreciate.

"I've had my life, Danny. I've actually been lucky enough to have had a couple of lives. That's how I see it. My body, however, apparently has a dissenting opinion." She gives me that old rueful smile of hers that reminds me of how she always looks when she comes to the waiting room to tell me to come in. "You're a guilty pleasure for me. You know that. I never meant to be involved with you. But that's all right, we're involved, I can't argue with that. And I also know that I owe you this conversation. But I have to be blunt here. Making a life with anybody else is completely out of the question for me. I'm not going to do that again. Even if that were possible—which it isn't, I assure you—I wouldn't choose you, Danny. I don't even like you."

Claire's hand goes up to her mouth. So I know she's said more than she meant to. She can't take it back. We're stuck with those words of hers being right out here between us. And I'm feeling like she just picked up an old-fashioned schoolteacher's paddle and swatted me across the chest with it. It's one of those times in my life when the feelings take over. I don't want my eyes to be welling up, and I don't want to let the sound out of my chest that comes out, but these things are happening anyway. I'm trying to remember the last time it was that I did this. It's got to be seventh or eighth grade or maybe even further back. To her credit, Claire stays put in her chair and keeps looking me straight in the face. If she touched me or looked away, I know I'd get up and walk out. She stays still. And in a moment she's crying, too.

"Reminds me of that Ray Stevens song," I manage to say. I dig in my hip pocket for my handkerchief. "This guy's in divorce court, talking to the judge. 'I been married four times, your honor,' he says. 'I'm not gonna do that no more. I'm just gonna go out and find myself a woman I hate and buy her a house.'"

Then Claire and I are both sort of half snorting, though maybe it's more crying than it is laughing.

"I didn't know I was going to say that, Danny," she says.

I shake my head and wave my hand to try to make her know that even though what she said matters more than anything, it doesn't really matter, which is something I know I can't say out loud. "I already know what you're telling me, Claire," I say. "If I were you, I wouldn't like me much either. I've always paid too much attention to women. In high school I was the guy girls wanted to dance with at parties. Or if they were having a fight with their boyfriend, I was the guy they wanted to go out with and maybe even fool around with—if they wanted to hurt the guy really bad. But no girl with good sense ever wanted to go steady with me. The ones that did I dropped after a week or two."

Claire stares at her lap and nods. "So even if I told you right now that I thought we ought to try to—" Her voice cracks a little. She makes herself go on. "Then you'd get what you want from me? And then next week you'd drop me?"

I stand up and walk around behind the sofa and in among her clusters of houseplants. I stand there looking out at the dark, the flakes of snow coming down, and the lights from this little slab of Bennington that her bay windows give me to see. "My timing isn't the same as it was in high school, Claire," I tell her. Now it's my turn to keep my back to her.

The silence holds. While I'm standing here looking out, I realize that I can actually see Claire behind me in the reflection of the window. I can't make out her features because her face is shadowed, but I can see how she sits there, how she's holding her shoulders straight while she stares at my back.

"You know what, Claire?" I say to her reflection. I jut my chin out toward the window, because all of a sudden now some attitude has come into me. I'm wanting to make a little speech to somebody, and it might as well be to Claire's reflection. "There may be more to me than just—" I pause, but I don't hear anything from Claire. "That's all I have to say," I say. "There may be more to me."

When I turn and face her, it's her turn to shake her head and wave her hand. "There may be less to me, Danny. I've shocked myself with what a sexual person I am. I've been thinking about this a lot lately. I'm one of those people who can remember all the way back into early childhood, and this particular event has been coming back to me. When I was six years old, I became extremely interested in the boy who delivered the afternoon paper to our house. He was maybe eleven or twelve at the time, and he was very handsome and friendly. Peter Firkens was his name. His parents were friends of my parents, and so it was natural for me to speak to him. I was just shameless in my flirtation. I'd wait for him on the porch. When he came along, I'd sing out, 'Hi, Peter Firkens.'

And he'd sing out, 'Hi, little Thompson girl.' And I'd sit down on the porch steps and try to persuade him that I wasn't a little girl. What I passionately wanted was for him to sit out there with me and talk. I wanted him to sit down beside me on the porch steps, and I wanted it so much it made me dizzy.

"Sometimes Peter would stand a minute or two and grin at me and say that even though he could see I wasn't a baby anymore, I still seemed like a pretty little girl to him. He had a baseball cap, which he'd sometimes take off while he stood there. Once he took the cap off and wiped the sweat from his brow with his wrist. God, did I love that! In my room, in front of the mirror, I imitated him doing that with his wrist again and again.

"My mother and father were much amused by my romantic obsession with our paperboy, but they were kind enough to go easy with their teasing me about it. For my seventh birthday, my mother decided to invite Peter Firkens to a surprise lunch for me. Some kids my own age were coming over later in the afternoon for a real party, and I knew about that, but this lunch was her secret present to me. I think she did it as a sign to me that she took Peter's place in my life—which was enormous—seriously.

"Peter accepted the invitation and agreed to keep it a secret to make the surprise part of it work. He was a nice boy, and he was very much at ease with both my parents. That day my mother had me getting dressed upstairs—I forget what excuse she used to make me put on my nice clothes early. She called me down for lunch, and when I went into the kitchen, there was Peter in a white shirt and a tie and holding a wrapped-up present for me.

"Have you ever read those accounts of people who've encountered angels? I think my response was like that. I wanted to flatten myself on the floor in front of him, and I wanted to run for my life—all at the same time. What I actually did was step back and give my mother this horrified expression; I needed her to explain to me how this thing had happened. When Peter moved toward me to hand me the present, I ran.

"My mother came and got me and persuaded me that Peter's feelings would be hurt if I didn't come back and be nice to him. With her holding my hand, I made it back to the kitchen. I even took the present from Peter and unwrapped it—it was a plastic tea set that I thought his mother must have picked out for him to give me. But I couldn't make myself look directly at him. It wasn't because I didn't want to. The one direct glimpse I'd had of him in his white shirt and tie was a glorious vision. Even his hair had been wetted down and combed in a much neater fashion than I'd ever seen it.

"We sat down to my favorite lunch—Campbell's tomato and rice soup and my mother's grilled-cheese sandwiches. I couldn't eat. I couldn't talk. I couldn't even let go of my mother's hand.

"So Peter and my mother had to make conversation, which I know wasn't easy for them. Neither of them had thought that I would be this way. They kept making openings for me, even addressing me directly with questions. But all I could do was stare at my plate and shake or nod my head and clasp my mother's hand even more tightly.

"In retrospect I know that lunch couldn't have lasted more than about forty-five minutes. At the time, it seemed to go on and on. And here is the thing I mean to tell you about it, Danny. It was joyful, and it was excruciating. Both at the same time. It was a magnified version of what I'd wanted from Peter Firkens, for him to sit down with me on the porch steps in the afternoon sun and to talk with me. But to have us both dressed up the way we were and inside my house and at my family's kitchen table with my favorite lunch on the table in front of us—it was just way too much for me. My face was hot. My body felt like it was just going to float away from me.

"I held onto my mother's hand all the way through the moment when Peter stepped out our kitchen door and waved goodbye to us. I waved to him, but I couldn't even say good-bye aloud. When he was gone, I ran up to my room and slammed the door and had the most magnificent cry of my life, a fair portion of it with my mother knocking on the door and asking me if she could please come in.

"Later on, when my friends showed up for the real party, I was wired. I chattered nonstop. I played the games my mother had planned for us like a little witch. I ripped open my presents. I blew out all seven candles in one huge whoosh of breath, then I wolfed down angel-food cake and strawberry ice cream. I can laugh about it now, but only a little bit."

I'm wondering if Claire is telling me why she got involved with me in the first place or why it just can't ever work out for us. But I'm not about to ask her what she means. At any rate, it's evident she likes what she's told me. So I lean back on the sofa, and the two of us sit there looking affectionately at each other. I don't mind the silence now.

"Our hour's up, Dr. McClelland," I finally say, standing up and stretching. "I think this has been a very productive session. Shall we plan on meeting next week at this same time?"

Claire shakes her head and smiles up at me. She's saying no, but she's nice enough not to say it out loud.

"I was kidding," I tell her. I keep my voice low and easy, but I'm feeling a clamor in my chest as I ask her, "Tomorrow morning at ten?" If she says no now, these may be the last moments I ever spend in her company.

Claire thinks about it only a moment. "Come at ten tomorrow," she says. "We'll see what happens."

I nod. I know then how it's going to be, how it has to be. I'm going to show up in the waiting room and wait for her as usual. She's going to come out and look at me and make up her mind whether to say, "Come in, Danny," or to shake her head at me and purge me from her life. She's going to make her mind up when she looks me in the face. That's how she's got to do it. And me? I know I've got to show up here in the morning and wait for her. If she tells me to come in, I'll walk past her—with a rueful smile of my own—and go in. If she shakes her head, I'll turn my back on her and get out of there fast. In ten minutes' time I'll be on the phone to some woman who'll be glad to hear from me. That's how I've got to do it. I don't have a choice. Christ, we're pitiful creatures, Claire and I.

That's what I'm thinking when all of a sudden I realize that she and I are moving through the strangest choreography. I've brought my coat into the office with me, and so we don't have to go back out to the waiting area. Instead, she's leading me through the building's old kitchen. We're not talking, but I understand what she wants me to do. There's a door back here that leads out to the private parking lot behind the building. When she opens that door for me, I step out, figuring she'll give me a wave from inside the building. But when I turn, she's walked with me outside into the snow. "You'll be cold," I say. "Your hair's going to get wet," I murmur. I reach toward her as if I could keep her from getting snowed on.

Claire doesn't say anything. She just lifts her arms. It's her good-bye hug, but the smell of her hair and her skin pumps me up, makes me feel like the circus strong man. I pick her up and spin us slowly around in the empty parking spaces. She's so light that I can't help showing off. On the snowed-over asphalt, I make waltz-step footprints. Claire holds me like I'm a scary ride she got on by accident. But that's all right. I'm careful with her, and I can go on like this for a long time.

Wherever I Am Not

~~~~~

Across a field of complete darkness, his eyes have fetched up these red digits from the clock on his dresser: 5:10. Was he sleeping with his eyes open? Maybe waking this morning was merely a matter of his mind's finally taking note of data his retinas had been transmitting for many minutes. Thoughts that come to Ben Mc-Clelland at this time of day often oddly please him.

Claire lies on her side, facing him and breathing deeply. She doesn't snore, but her breathing at night is a strong sifting sound that took Ben some weeks to get used to. She's his second wife; he's her second husband. He's forty-six; she's thirty-seven. They are so affectionate, so tender with each other that Ben doubts it's romantic love they're feeling. Sex isn't usually what he wants, but he can't get enough of being around Claire. His mind works at defining how it was that he felt about his first wife at this point in their marriage. What he and Julie felt for each other was what someone would feel about possessing a rare and supernaturally sharp knife—thrilled, proud, and excited, but also scared. As much as Julie enraged and frightened him, he nevertheless always desired her. On a couple of occasions he thinks they made love to avoid hitting each other with their fists. He releases a small prayer of thanks that he ended that first marriage without doing physical harm to Julie.

Who is it I'm thanking? he wonders at the point where he knows the Amen should come.

No god Ben could believe in would be interested in receiving little prayers like the one he just transmitted. Ben is annoyed by his inclination to pray, especially when he wants or needs something. He sees himself as a kid whining for a candy bar at the spiritual grocery store checkout. He's certain prayer has to be cleaner than that. Disinterested. In this case, he's pleased at the unselfish nature of his prayer of thanks, but he's still disturbed at his impulse to pray when he has no proper address for his prayers.

Ben has never personally experienced the grandeur of prayer. Nor has he known anyone who spoke about it in such a way that he believed that person had experienced it. Even so, he suspects there is a grandeur out there to which he has always been—and likely always will be—denied access. "Out there": his mind plays with the concept. Does he mean "outer space"? Or does he mean anywhere he isn't?

Such religious beliefs as Ben subscribes to are vaguely scientific—creation and life ultimately explainable in terms of physics and biology. He doesn't go for a humanlike—and most especially not for a fatherlike—god. On the other hand, the patterns discernible in creation and nature incline him toward something like faith. The way fish in a school or blackbirds in a flock simultaneously change direction, the arrangements of leaves in a tree, rock and sky and cloud and water—all those intricate patterns persuade Ben that some kind of a pattern-maker is or was "out there." (*Anywhere I am not*, his mind whispers to him.) Creation appears to him not randomly flung. Most likely the pattern-maker is mere astrophysics.

In their two years of marriage—and the year of their acquaintance before their marriage—Ben and Claire have discussed religion only briefly and superficially. Ben knows he has no plans to discuss it with Claire, no desire to do so now or anytime in the future. So is this my secret life? he wonders with a slight smile. What kind of a husband keeps his thoughts about prayer a secret from his wife? He makes his way quietly up out of bed.

Ben pees, showers, shaves, brushes his teeth, and puts on the clean underwear he set out on the clothes hamper last night. Then he brushes his hair and moves closer to the mirror to see what it will show him this morning. He tries to see himself as Claire would see him. Claire likes sitting this close to him on the sofa or moving over him in bed to study his face. She will brush away a flake of skin or push and prod this place and that; if he will tolerate it, she will even squeeze a blackhead on his nose. Ben likes the closeness of Claire as well as the sensation of her fingers on his face. He likes Claire's voice when they're right up next to each other, very low in her throat, as if she were humming to herself. When she's propped on her elbows over him in bed, he can feel her voice with his chest against hers. Once, when his arms were around her and she was murmuring that way, he had the sensation of holding this human musical instrument in his arms. "You are my Stradivarius, Claire," he told her. She gave him a look, but he wasn't sure she understood him. Now that he's thoroughly considered his face in the mirror, he can't imagine why she'd devote so many minutes to examining him. His face appears raw to him, so utterly revealing that he bugs his eyes and puffs his cheeks, then shuts off the light and goes out into the hallway.

It is in this part of this house and at this time of day that Ben always thinks of Meg, his and Julie's daughter. It's utterly dark here. Ben brushes the wall with the fleshy heel of his hand to keep himself oriented and glides through the dark passage to the guest room. To keep from bothering Claire with his getting dressed, that's where each night he sets out his clothes for the next day. In the old house, in his previous life, one morning when Meg was around thirteen and going through her most difficult phase, Ben had been walking through the hallway in the dark like this and had heard Meg call out, "Ahhehlilmmnnooozs-hargh!" He had stopped instantly and stood still, both frightened and comforted by the phrase called out from the world of Meg's dream. She seemed to have spoken directly to him in a language he didn't know. The remark had seemed a spirited one, entirely lacking in the anger that in recent months had tinged so much of what Meg had to say to Ben. He had stood there in the total dark until he lost all sense of his body, trying to think what Meg might be dreaming, trying to translate what she had said. He thought it was like being spoken to by the dead. Then he thought that Meg's voice was so enlivened, and his own circumstance—of standing in the dark hallway—was so metaphysically dubious, that he must be the dead one. So this was what it was like for the dead to hear their loved ones addressing them across the great barrier.

In the guest room, Ben turns on a light by which to find his clothes and get dressed. He thinks that it's perverse how, now that Meg is grown—she's twenty-one—and just about to finish college and go out on her own, her health has become precarious. The last time she called him from school, she said, "I don't feel good, Dad. I just don't feel good. I don't know what it is." The doctor at the college infirmary has suggested to Meg that the way she feels may be more a matter of senior anxiety than of anything's being physically wrong with her. But Ben's worried about her. As he ties his shoes this morning, *Let Meg be well* escapes his lips in a whisper—a determined little prayer bursting loose like that, he thinks, floating "out there" with no acceptable address. And he himself, the one who released the prayer, must be a *pray-er*, or a *prayist*—maybe that's what he is, an incorrigible *prayist*.

All his adult life, Ben has gone to bed early and gotten up before anyone else. His system for moving through this house is almost exactly the same as the one he had for the old place he lived in with Julie and Meg. After he makes that one passage through the dark, moving each morning from the bathroom to the guest room, he wants there to be light ahead of him. Thus, now, with his left hand, he switches off the light in the guest room, while simultaneously with his right hand he reaches around the doorjamb for the switch to the light in the downstairs hallway. Executing this maneuver pleases him. An old fear of his is of encountering an intruder in the dark, actually running into another human body, one that intends to harm him. Ben doesn't know the origin of this fear. He's never had anything terribly unpleasant happen to him in the dark; he's never encountered an intruder anywhere he's ever lived. In the army, he was taught a systematic way to move through the dark in enemy territory. It was a slow-motion, modern-dance kind of movement that he remembers so clearly he could perform it perfectly right now, but like most of what he learned in the army—saluting, spit-shining shoes, reading a map, zeroing in a rifle, executing the nine jump commands—it's a skill that's of no use to him in his current life.

There are times when Ben wishes he could trade in all the useless knowledge he's got stored up in his brain; he could use some fresh material—new stuff that he'd really enjoy knowing. What would that new knowledge be? Maybe information about animals and computers, maybe things about Claire and about Meg and— he can hardly stand to admit this to himself—about Julie. The thought jolts him right in the middle of pouring coffee beans into the shiny mouth of the grinder. Why, of all things, does he want to know more than he knows—which is an astonishing amount of data—about Julie? Julie who hates his guts? Julie who generated more misery in his life than all his other sources of misery put together? Julie who made him feel—as she so memorably phrased it for him in one of their 39,000 arguments—like a squashed pissant on the outer shores of Mongolia? Ben shakes the buzzing little machine as if it held some potion he could use to purge himself of all the unpleasant memories he holds of his first marriage.

There's a notion that's about to come into Ben's mind; he can feel it approaching, but he doesn't want it to arrive. He searches his mental files for another topic to engage his interest, something to fend off this hostile idea. But it's the exact wrong time of the morning for him to be able to locate an effective distraction. The coffee's brewing. The teakettle is on. (Before he pours his coffee, Ben heats up his cup with boiling water—he's become so fastidious about this routine that the only place he can enjoy coffee is here at home.) Ordinarily, what he does during these minutes of waiting for the coffee is take the dishes out of the dish drainer, wipe off the stove and the countertop, straighten up the kitchen, and check the houseplants to see if they need watering. He knows that while he putters around like this, his mind meanders. So this

morning he stands still, his butt propped against the kitchen counter, his arms crossed in front of him, his head bowed. Whether
he wants it or not, this thought has injected itself into his brain: he
wants to call Julie. He wants to call Julie immediately.

Pouring his coffee, another little prayer escapes Ben's mind:
Let me not call Julie. He'd be amused by this one except that now he's
filled with dread. It's taken him half his lifetime to reach the point
of being completely free of Julie. When Meg turned 21, it became
officially the case that there was no further need for them to communicate. Ben supposes that if and when Meg gets married, he
and Julie will have to have some sort of exchange. But after he and
Claire got married, Ben worked with the lawyers to refine the divorce contract to such an extent that he and Julie never had to
speak or write directly to each other. It was one of their few points
of agreement; Julie claimed she wanted to talk with him even less
than he wanted to talk with her.

On the sofa now, with his book in his lap, Ben calculates it
out—it has been more than thirteen months since he and Julie
last spoke to each other. That was in the Grand Union on Ira Allen
Road. He was kneeling down to reach on a bottom shelf for what
he wanted when a voice behind and above him (now that he was
on one knee) rasped at him, "Still buying that same old turd-
flavored coffee, huh, Ben?" When he looked behind him, Julie
was pushing her cart on up the aisle. He didn't say anything, just
watched her from his kneeling position. Sure enough, she turned
around to check to see if he was looking. She stuck her tongue out
at him, mouthed something—maybe called him a name—and
turned the corner of the aisle. That was the last Ben saw or heard
from Julie.

Ben has a couple of hours to read now. He's come to understand that this is the part of his day that will "set him right"—if
he is going to be "set right" today. He's the associate dean of the
college; his job requires six or seven hours of discussion a day, in
meetings or in conversations with the dean, his boss, and with fac-
ulty members and students. Ben is actually a professor of political
science, but some years ago, when he realized he wasn't going to
find a publisher for his book on legislative compromise, he made a

decision to move into the administration. It took him about six months of doing his associate dean's job to realize that the reason he felt so miserable all the time was that he wasn't reading anymore. The only reading a dean's job required was of reports, memos, and computer screens. When he went home in the evening, he was too tired to read anything more challenging than the newspaper. Something popped into focus: he couldn't do without reading. So he started getting up early enough in the morning to be able to spend a couple of hours with a book.

Now he's double- and triple-reading paragraphs of Howard Ball's biography of Justice Black, the book that yesterday morning he found so engrossing that he very nearly let Claire oversleep. Ben knows himself well enough to see he's not going to be able to disregard the thought that's come to him this morning. There's an excellent chance that if he calls Julie, she'll tell him to piss off, and that will be that, he won't have to be pestered with wondering what she might have to say to him.

The phone sits over on the table in the far corner. Beside it is an easy chair that's comfortable to sit in while talking on the phone. It's quarter after six now. Claire's time to wake up is seven-thirty. There's plenty of time for him to make the call. He tries to imagine what Julie might be doing now. Often she's awake and throwing pots at this time of day. Or sketching or writing in her journal. Or puttering around. But sometimes she sleeps late. Unless something absolutely requires her to pay attention to it, Julie disregards time. She's very cagey about making appointments. Ben used to think that she willed herself not to let time control her life and that she took pride in being that way. Now he knows he was wrong: Julie really is naturally inclined to live in a way Ben can't help but see as chaotic. She doesn't try to be that way; it's just who she is. This is what seems so urgently on Ben's mind this morning: Julie was never trying to devil him.

Ben knows his recent understanding would not have helped him live any more happily with Julie, but it might have prevented so much bitterness from evolving between them. Maybe that's what he's needing to tell her this morning. And he decides that's an okay reason for calling her. He moves over to the chair and dials the number he supposes he'll be carrying in his memory as long as he's got a memory to carry it.

"Julie here."

"Ben here."

This is old between them. Years ago, when he realized that she wouldn't ever say an ordinary hello answering the phone, he started copying whatever she did say. At the time he thought he might demonstrate her own oddness to her, but Julie took it as a little game between the two of them. It pleased her when he echoed her like that. She's chuckling now, which lets Ben know he didn't wake her.

"Ben, Ben, Bo Benny. First ring, I knew it was you."

"I haven't called you for a couple of years. How could you know it was me, Julie?" This is always the way it is: he thinks he's got perspective on their relationship; within four sentences, Julie's got his hackles up. Already he's having to remind himself to keep his voice low or he'll wake Claire.

"Either my mother died or it's you. It's morning and still dark outside, Benny. Who's gonna call me at this time of day except you? Don't be mad. Is it my fault I know you like I put you together myself? A couple of weeks ago I started knowing you were going to call me. But I know you don't like that either. What's up, darling? What's on your mind?"

This, too, is one of Julie's disconcerting mannerisms. They could be teeth-and-claws screaming at each other, and she'd call him darling. "Blow it out your ass, darling," she said in one of their worst arguments. Ben moves the receiver away from his face a moment and takes a deep breath. He reminds himself that Claire has never called him either darling or Benny and is not likely ever to tell him to blow it out his ass. For his own spiritual development, he thinks it's probably good that there's somebody in the world who'll speak to him like this.

"Have you heard from Meg lately?" Ben asks her.

Noises tell Ben that Julie is lighting a cigarette. "Still smoking, huh?" he says, though he'd take it back if he could. He certainly didn't call her after a two-year silence to nag about her smoking.

"Yes, I've heard from Meg lately, and yes, I'm still smoking. And I don't mind discussing either of those topics with you, Ben, but neither one of them made you pick up the phone and dial my number. So what will it be, small talk or get down to it?"

Ben can't make himself respond quickly enough. He hears her exhaling. "You don't know why you called, do you, Ben?" she murmurs in the low voice she usually uses to talk to herself.

Another pause comes that Ben knows he should fill with some words of his own, but he can't locate them.

"How much time before Claire wakes up?" Julie asks. Her voice is still soft. She isn't trying to antagonize him.

Ben makes a gesture with the hand that isn't holding the receiver to his ear. To say aloud what time Claire will wake up would be a betrayal of Claire.

"You still there, Benny? Surely you're not going to let the cat get your tongue. It'll be at least another couple of years before you get up the nerve to call me again."

Ben clears his throat. "I've been thinking," he says.

Julie chuckles. "Why am I not surprised to hear that, Ben? No wait, don't get mad. I'm sorry. I know this isn't easy for you, darling. I'm interested. I definitely want to know your thoughts. There. Can you tell me what you've been thinking, Ben?"

"I've been thinking that you weren't trying to get me upset. I've been thinking that it wasn't necessary for me to get so angry with you." Ben has forced himself to say these things. Now they seem to him raw, repulsive verbal constructions he has retched up.

Julie is quiet for a moment. "I'm surprised you would say that, Ben."

"You were just being the way you are," Ben says.

"Yes, that's true," Julie muses. But she doesn't go on.

"Surely you're not going to let the cat get your tongue," Ben says. He's pleased to have recovered enough poise to be able to tease her.

"I don't know, Ben. I mean I think it's very sweet of you to come up with these thoughts. But I'm trying to think about how true they really are."

"You mean you actually were trying to upset me?"

"Maybe so, Benny. I think now maybe I was, though back then I certainly didn't think so. I thought I was just being myself and so why were you getting so mad at me? Didn't you marry me? Didn't you marry me because you liked how I was? It always seemed crazy to me the way you got all worked up because I took Meg downtown and we were having a good time, and so we didn't get home when you thought we ought to be eating dinner. Remember how you were throwing things around in the kitchen?"

"Yes. That's what I'm talking about. You were just being yourself. You weren't trying to make me angry."

"I'm not sure."

"Julie!"

"You're not the only one who's been doing some thinking."

"What do you mean?"

"Well, for one thing, you know how I always acted like I was the mellow one, like I was the one who never got mad or upset about anything? Now I think I was actually furious at you the whole time we were married."

"You were mad at me, Julie?"

"The way you processed every thought you had before you said a word. You might as well have typed out your part of our conversations. And the way you cultivated habits. The way you loved those habits of yours. I hated those things about you. It was like living with a robot or a mannequin. The only time I ever got to see the truth of you was when you were mad. Maybe you were throwing my grandmother's cooking utensils around the kitchen, but at least you were showing me something real. Not making a remark that you'd been chewing on for three days before you delivered it up to me and Meg at the dinner table. And not polishing your cordovan plain toes because that's what you always did on Thursday mornings."

Ben can't say a thing. It actually makes him dizzy to have to think this way, to have to adjust his view of these thousands of days that he lived through with such a definite sense of how things were. All that time she seemed so calm, Julie was angry with him? Even when they were fighting, she always seemed to him the one whose emotions were under control. Ben guesses it must have been a very controlled form of rage she felt toward him, but right now it feels to him like sitting in his living room and sensing the whole house make a quarter turn on its foundation. *Let me get through this conversation* escapes his mind; he even mouths the word *conversation*.

"There's a thing I never told you, Benny."

"I don't know if this is a good time to tell me, Julie. I called you because I thought I had it all figured out about us." Ben is surprised at how much anguish is showing in his voice. "Now it turns out I had no idea. Now or then. I didn't know the first thing."

"Don't feel bad, darling. Nobody does. That's another little insight I got out of my thinking. Maybe we didn't understand exactly what we were living through. But who does? Well, I can't say that. Maybe there are some who get on top of it all and stay there. People tell me you and Claire are very happy."

"People talk about us? People tell you things about us?"

"God, Ben. What kind of a town do you think we're living in? Of course they tell me things. They tell me how much you ate at the Cochrans' St. Patrick's Day party. They tell me what Claire wore. Significant things like that. I keep hoping I'll get a report from underneath your bed covers, but so far it hasn't happened."

Ben clears his throat. He wonders if Julie is still mad at him and this is why she feels she has to embarrass him.

"Ben, I do need to tell you this thing. If you hadn't called me, I'd have had to call you. This is what came to me from doing all this thinking. It's become an obstacle in my life. I've got to get it out there."

"If you slept with somebody, I don't want to know about it. Keep it to yourself, Julie."

She doesn't answer him. Ben feels a sweat breaking out across his forehead.

"It was Roger Pendleton, wasn't it, Julie?" Roger Pendleton is an old high school pal of Julie's who keeps in touch with her, a loathsome man in Ben's opinion.

She still doesn't say anything, but Ben is determined to wait her out this time. Far in the background of the phone lines, he can hear a man drawling on and on about how intelligent his dog is. He keeps waiting for the other voice in that conversation to come on the line, but the drawling man never lets up. Maybe this is a man who has simply picked up a phone receiver somewhere in America and begun telling it the story of his life with his dog.

She says something.

"What, Julie? I can't understand you."

"Elliott Barkley."

"Elliott Barkley?"

"He's the one I slept with."

Ben is relieved. He knows Julie is lying. "Julie, maybe you slept with him in your dreams, but you can't have done it in real life. We were too close to them. We were around them all the time. Elliott and I spent hours and hours together. I'd have known it if you were sleeping with him."

The receiver makes no sound.

"Julie, I even had a fantasy or two about Katie Barkley. That was natural. But it just didn't happen. It didn't happen with me and Katie, and it didn't happen with you and Elliott."

In the silence, a little prayer breaks loose from Ben. *Don't let this be!*

"You remember there were some nights when you were tired and went to bed and let me walk Salter? Katie was like you in that regard, you remember. On weeknights she went to bed early, too, if we weren't over there keeping them up. If I walked the dog, where else would I walk him except down in that little park at Riverside and 102nd where the Barkleys always walked their Casey? If Elliott and I got to talking down there in Riverside, wouldn't he have invited me in for a cup of tea? You remember that Elliott and I both loved Constant Comment?"

"Julie, Elliott wasn't like that. He wasn't a sneak. Neither are you, for that matter. But Elliott was a completely up-front guy. He and I talked about everything. I told Elliott things about my life that I never even told you."

A bit of silence passes before Julie begins speaking again. "You remember how the Barkleys' apartment was set up with their bedroom in back and a hallway for the bathroom door on one side and Katie's sewing room on the other, and then a living room, then a dining room, then the kitchen? So if you were in one end of it, you couldn't hear what was going on in the other end of it, right?"

"Julie, Katie and Elliott were the happiest married couple you and I ever met. We used to point to them as the exception when we were listing off all the couples we knew who were miserable. Katie and Elliott adored each other."

Again there's a pause before Julie goes on. "Salter and Casey, as you know, were inclined to romp all over the apartment when they were in there together, and you remember the way Elliott would put them in the dining room and close the door, and that way they could play in there and not bother us when we were in the living room?"

"Julie—"

"Ben, be quiet. I know this is hard for you to hear. It's not easy for me to tell you. I need you just to shush for a little while. So here we are, Elliott and I are in the kitchen with our Constant Comment. Katie's asleep in the other end of the apartment. Salter and Casey are in the dining room, winding down the way they used to do when they finally got tired, with their tongues lolling out and panting at each other. And you remember how Elliott is such a hands-on kind of guy. You and I even talked about it, how he doesn't mean anything, it's just the way he relates to people, by touching them.

"So I'm sitting up on the kitchen counter, and he's standing there right beside me, and we're sipping our Constant Comment, and we're really enjoying what we're talking about. It's a movie, as I'm sure you would have guessed. It's actually *The New Centurions*. And Elliott is quoting me that line that later on you and he used to say back and forth to each other, 'The street's full of assholes.' Elliott puts his hand up on my shoulder—you can see him doing that, he does it to people all the time. And then, just as he's taking away his hand, he brushes my cheek very lightly with his fingertips."

There's another pause, but Ben isn't tempted to say a word. He wishes he had a word disintegrator, like the weapons heroes use in computer games to obliterate obstacles and enemies. He'd blast away these words of Julie's as they came sifting out of the receiver.

"This is the really hard part, Ben. The rest of it is kind of interesting, but this is the part I feel bad about. As he was pulling it away, I grabbed Elliott's hand and held onto it and looked him in the eye. At the moment, I didn't know if I was confronting him or just wanting confirmation that he'd done what he'd done. But I think that's what tipped the balance. If I hadn't grabbed his hand, Elliott wouldn't have gone any further than touching my cheek. But I did grab it. So I'm sitting on the counter, and he's standing right there in front of me, and I'm holding on, and we're staring into each other's faces. That's when he says, 'I just like you guys so much.' It was like there it was, that was the contract.

"That was a strange thing for him to say, really. But then the whole situation moved from perfectly normal right into the middle of crazyland. As easy as could be. We kissed—and even that could have started out as a friendly act. But then we just went up in flames. It was awkward in that kitchen, but that couldn't have mattered less to us. I got the impression that Elliott and Katie had done it in that kitchen a few times, because he definitely knew how to engineer it. But the whole time, it was like this passionate act of friendship. It was like Elliott and I were doing it, but we were also doing it for you and Katie. Just from his having said what he said.

"I know. I know it's crazy. It always seemed that way to me, too, when I wasn't right there with him. But whenever I thought about it, I always went back to that thing Elliott said. If he'd said, 'Julie, I've got to have you,' or 'Julie, I love you,' or anything that made it just him and me, I think I'd have turned it off. But he made it this expression of what he and I felt for the four of us. We all got so close. And I kept thinking it was because of what Elliott and I were doing. The even crazier thing is that it was true. We never would have gotten as close as we did without Elliott and me screwing. Elliott was just so nice to you. I was the same to Katie. I guess it was guilt that made us that way toward the two of you, but it was also the intimacy Elliott and I had that made it possible for us to be so nice to you and Katie. I don't know. I know there were times, especially when the four of us were together, when I was really, deeply happy."

"How many times did you and Elliott do it?" Ben hates how his voice rasps saying this.

"I don't expect you to understand it. I wouldn't understand it either if you told me something like this."

"I understand it perfectly well, Julie. Just tell me how many times. I'm sorry, but it's something I seem to need to know."

Julie is quiet so long that Ben thinks she isn't going to answer him at all. Finally, she says, "Thirty-two."

A long silence passes that seems full of content. Ben clears his throat. "This was a long time ago, Julie," he says.

"Yes."

"I guess it hurts anyway. I don't know. I think that's what I'm feeling. But maybe it's more because of Elliott than because of you. I thought he was my friend. I thought he was the one friend I had in the world. I thought I could call him up anytime and trust him with anything."

"But you haven't called him in a long time."

"You have?"

"Yes."

"What's going on?"

"Not what you think. I'd been thinking about you and me and thinking about those days in New York. Except for when Salter died, and I called the Barkleys to tell them about that, Elliott and I hadn't been in touch at all since you and I left the city. But when I got to doing all this thinking about you and me, I had to ask Elliott what he thought about what happened between him and me and whether or not I ought to tell you."

"What did he think?"

"He didn't want me to tell you. He says he and I were in another zone when we did that. 'Some other dimension of time and space' was his phrase. He says it doesn't even count. He says he's never going to tell Katie. And he says he wouldn't ever do anything like that again."

"Maybe I should give Katie a call."

"You want me to ask you not to?"

"Oh, I don't know, Julie. I don't know." Ben realizes he's about to cry, and he doesn't think it's because he's angry or hurt by what Julie's told him. It feels like something bigger than that. "I think I must be having a really hard time of it here lately." He means to offer this to Julie by way of explaining why he's in the state he's in, but it comes through his voice as a wailing into the phone receiver. "I'm sorry," he says. Then he says, "I sometimes get this feeling that I've lost my whole life. Like I wasn't paying attention the way I should have been, and it just got snatched right away from me."

The silence of the phone receiver doesn't bother him. He's glad Julie gives him a moment or two to get himself back together. Finally, she does speak up. "Anybody would tell you, Ben, try to talk to Claire. Talk it out. That's what you need to do. Here's what else I can tell you. When we were married, you never would have talked to me about anything like this. And look what happened to us."

"What are you saying, Julie?"

"I'm saying it's one thing to whisper your soul into a phone receiver in a dark room with your ex-wife on the other end of the line and another thing to speak it straight out in broad daylight to the person you live with."

"Excuse me, but—"

"Excuse you, but you're not the one who just dumped this huge confession on your ex. I know, I know, Benny. You and I never are going to get it all balanced out, are we? I was so glad when you called. I thought now we had this chance to close the books on us. I thought we could have this talk, then I could stop falling into a trance in the middle of driving to Williamstown worrying about whether or not you were trying to make Claire worship your habits the way you did me. I could stop worrying about why you could never understand why it didn't make a pig's foot of difference whether we ate dinner at 6:30 or 7:30."

"Do you really do that, Julie?"

"No, Ben. I don't do that." Julie laughs. "One other thing. Don't worry about Meg. Meg is afraid she's going to lose both her parents when she graduates from college. She's like a kid who feels too sick to go to school but who actually just needs to stay at home a day to be reassured that her parents really do care about her. Go up there and take her out to lunch and listen to her problems. Give her a big hug and tell her you love her. That'll get her through most of this spring term."

"What if she really does turn out to be gravely ill?"

"I'll be sorry I didn't take her more seriously. I'll never trust my intuition again. I'll call you up and apologize for having given you bad advice. I'll try to quit smoking again. I'll—"

"Okay, Julie. Okay." She's done it again, gotten him riled up with her stupid routines. But it's just a quick burst of anger that flashes through him; it doesn't last. Through the window by his chair, Ben sees daylight is arriving in his backyard. He suddenly feels as tired as if he'd just finished some rigorous task of manual labor like chopping wood or doing a day's worth of yard work. "Julie, I—"

Julie doesn't say anything.

"Julie, I'm not sure what it is, but I feel like I have something important to tell you before we hang up."

"I wonder what it is." Her voice has a low, interested tone, the way it was on those rare occasions they were in sync with each other, trying to figure something out together. "You'd think we'd both said it all by now."

"The great speeches Ben and Julie have made to each other across a quarter of a century." Ben is amazed that he can suddenly drop into this mode of kidding around with Julie, their old looking-back-on-it-wryly way of teasing things back to normal.

"Do you think it was about Elliott and me, something about that?"

"I don't know, Julie. It's a lot to process. Right now I feel a little of this, a little of that. And we're not married anymore. So what difference does it make what I feel about it? I guess if I ever see Elliott again, I'll try to make myself bust him one across the chops. But you know me. I'm not the most aggressive guy. Maybe when I see him, I'll just ask, 'What did you think of her, Elliott? How was she?'"

Ben listens to Julie lighting a cigarette, inhaling, then exhaling and speaking at the same time. "You know what it is about you?" Her voice is slightly muffled by the tobacco smoke that seeps through her throat along with the words. "You're an emotional mole. This is something else I figured out. You might occasionally encounter somebody else—like your wife or your daughter— and feel a little something, but mostly what you want to do is go off by yourself and tunnel away at whatever it is that's going on inside you. Tunnel away all by yourself in the dark. You don't want to get out there in the daylight, and you definitely don't want to get next to anybody else and stay with them. And you don't want anybody else down there in the tunnel with you."

"Does this go down as another one of Julie's great speeches?"

"I guess it does."

"What was it Meggie used to say to us when we were on her case? 'It's not my fault I'm like I am.'"

Now it's Julie's turn to chuckle. "Yes, that's what she said, and not only that, the way she said it, clearly she meant that it was our fault she was the way she was. If she did something wrong, it was our fault."

"So do you suppose I can blame it on you—my being an emotional mole?"

"Just don't go thinking somebody else stole your life from you, Ben. That's all I'm saying."

"I wasn't accusing you, Julie."

"I know. I know, Benny. Christ, here we are again. It's like a chemical reaction with us, you know that?"

"I guess I'd better get moving around here, Julie. But you know what's been happening to me lately that I can't quite figure out? I've been praying. Little prayers flare up out of me. Like this morning I prayed for Meg to be okay. Do you think I'm in danger of getting religion?"

"Yeah, you might be. Keep an eye on yourself, Ben. Remember what I told you."

"What was that?"

"Talk to Claire."

"Talk to Claire, right." Ben is about to go on when he realizes that Julie is not on the line anymore. He takes the receiver away from his ear and looks at it. "Did you just hang up on me?" he asks it. But then he can envision Julie—maybe even doing it absent-mindedly—setting the receiver down and moving across the room to do something she just thought of doing. "I guess we're finished talking, huh?" he says, setting the receiver in its cradle. He gets up from the chair and goes back to the sofa where his book is. "Talk to Claire," he says.

Ben opens the biography of Justice Black again, but this time he doesn't even pretend to himself to be reading it. He just stares at it while he replays his conversation with Julie. The image that lingers in his mind is of Katie Barkley asleep in her bedroom with Elliott entertaining Julie in the kitchen. Ben finds it oddly distressing that he knows Katie usually sleeps on her side with her arms around a pillow. He has some dim memory of Elliott's telling him about finding Katie hugging her pillow and smiling in her sleep and how he couldn't help wondering what was going on in her dreams. When the clock tells Ben it's time to pour Claire's coffee and carry it up to her, he finds he's been transported back to the years he and Julie spent living on West End Avenue while he finished up his graduate work at Columbia.

Claire is easily startled from sleep. Her former husband terrorized her in such a way that often when Ben brings her her coffee, she jerks awake as if she's certain she's about to be assaulted. She said Jim Boscowen actually hit her only a couple of times in all their years together, but what he liked to do when he was drunk was make her flinch; he'd draw back his hand as if he were going to slap her. Another of his amusements was scaring her awake. Claire has assured Ben that he's to ignore the way she wakes up now—her fears are quickly dispelled, and she is, as she puts it, "so relieved that I'm okay and not married to Jim anymore that it actually feels good." But when Ben is responsible for making her gasp and shoot upright in bed, it's as if he's been wrongly accused. It troubles him for hours afterward. He wishes there were such a clear distinction in her mind between himself and Jim Boscowen

that in her first instant out of sleep, Claire would recognize the difference. Lately, he's discovered a method of waking Claire that pre-
vents startling her. In the now dimly lit hallway, as he approaches
the bedroom with Claire's cup of coffee and the newspaper, he
begins softly singing to her: "Oh, Claire—oh, pretty Cla-aire—I'm
bringing you your cof-fee—and your news-paper—fresh from
the front porch—it's ti-ime to wa-ake up—and here you ah-are."

It works this morning. Though it's too dark to see her, he
hears Claire stirring in bed as he sets the newspaper beside her and
fumbles for the switch on the bedside lamp. "Good morning, my
dear," he says in the blast of light. She's stretching and smiling at
him, a sight that pleases him. "Morning," she says. Usually after
only a few pleasantries, Ben leaves Claire to her paper and heads
back downstairs to his book. She's fuzzy-headed for the first half
hour or so of her waking; he finds it frustrating to be so out of
sync with her when he's been up for hours with his mind thoroughly quickened by coffee. This morning, though, after opening
a set of curtains, he takes a seat in the one chair they keep in the
bedroom. "Claire, I—," he begins.

Claire looks at him. She has plumped up her pillows behind
herself as she likes them, and she has the newspaper resting on her
lap. Ben understands that he wants to tell Claire about his conversation with Julie. He understands that to Claire it may be uncom-
monly significant that he has called Julie. She may require him to
explain at length. He understands that if he doesn't tell Claire that
he just talked to Julie, he will be deliberately deceiving her. Her
expression is friendly, interested, none too alert. A little prayer
whispers its way out of him: *Let me say the right thing.*

"Claire, I just talked with Julie." All he has to do is keep going,
but something stops him.

"You called her?" Her eyes flick into focus on his face; he
knows she's alert now.

Ordinarily, Ben forgets all about Claire's being a psycholo-
gist. But now, he warns himself to watch what he says. She brings
some expertise to this conversation. Most of her clients are men
and women dealing with divorce. "I got to worrying about Meg."
He forces calmness into his voice and feels relieved that he's telling

the truth. "I thought Julie might have some insight about what Meg's going through down at school."

"Did she?"

"Yes, she did. She says Meg is afraid she's going to lose her parents when she graduates. She told me to go up there and take her out to lunch and give her a hug and tell her that I love her."

"Good advice." Ben can actually see Claire's level of interest diminishing. She smiles at him, then lets her eyes drift down toward the newspaper lying on her lap. She raises it halfway toward reading position as she says, "Julie was up?"

"She was up," Ben says. "But you never know with Julie. She never does two things twice the same way. Tomorrow morning I could call her at the same time and wake her from a deep sleep. She was actually in a pretty good mood this morning."

Claire has raised the paper and is letting her eyes take in the headlines. "Oh?" she says.

"We got to talking about when we lived in New York. When we had that golden retriever named Salter? We had these friends who lived on Riverside Drive—we met them through walking our dog in the park. The Barkleys. They had a dalmatian named Casey."

"Um."

Ben can see that Claire's attention has begun to drift completely away from him and what he is telling her. He could at this instant say, *Julie just told me she slept with Elliott Barkley, my best friend,* and he would recover every bit of Claire's awareness. If he did that, she would set the newspaper aside and give him a level of concern he knows he doesn't want right now. Claire would concentrate on helping him. But he doesn't see himself as exactly working through a problem.

So as Claire makes the transition from scanning the paper to actually reading the front-page articles, Ben hears himself telling about the time Salter and Casey were romping through the Barkleys' apartment and got into Katie's sewing room. "We were sitting in the living room, chatting away, when we heard this enormous clattering back in there, like somebody was moving furniture, and both dogs began barking. Then the clattering started moving toward us with the dogs coming with it. It was spooky.

We were all four just about halfway standing up when Salter and Casey came charging into the living room with Katie's ironing board banging up through the hallway behind them, the dogs running away from it and barking like all hell had broken loose. It made no sense whatsoever. The ironing board was chasing the dogs. Then Elliott figured it out. We hadn't unhooked Salter's leash from his collar, and it had gotten caught on the foot of the ironing board. So Salter couldn't get away from it. The more it followed him the more freaked out he got. And Casey, too, even though he wasn't attached to it. Elliott caught Salter and set him free, but the four of us went on laughing about what we thought when we saw those dogs come barreling out of the hallway pursued by the ironing board—"

"Um."

"It was probably the funniest two or three minutes I've ever lived through."

Claire smiles at him. "I wish I could have seen it," she says.

For a moment Ben imagines himself in the Barkleys' living room visiting Katie and Elliott just as in the old days except with both Julie and Claire. He's sitting on the Barkleys' living-room sofa with one wife on each side of him. It's such an unsettling vision that now in his own bedroom he stands up rather more suddenly than he intended. Then, for poise, he puts his hands in his pockets and smiles at Claire. "Just as well you weren't," he says. "I doubt you'd have liked the Barkleys. Julie and I used to smoke pot with them. It was an early seventies New York thing. Have an elegant dinner and smoke a couple of joints before dessert." Ben is moving toward the door as he speaks.

"Somehow I can't imagine you doing that." Claire turns the page of the newspaper. "My husband, the pothead," she says.

"I did it," Ben says. "I was the man. I was there," he murmurs as he walks down the hallway. He's surprised he feels so relieved. *Thanks for letting me get by with that* floats out of his consciousness. But at the top of the steps, Ben suddenly stops and stands with one hand on the wall the way he does when it's dark and he's feeling his way. *What did I just get by with?* he asks himself. *Exactly what was I hiding from Claire?*

These questions hover in his mind, but no satisfactory answers occur to Ben throughout the rest of the morning. He sits a bit longer with the biography of Justice Black in his lap and even reads a few paragraphs, but intermittently he has this sensation that is like an inner sweating—as if his spirit has suffered some embarrassment or humiliation. Through the ceiling he hears Claire getting up and stirring around. Then he hears her shower water running. He hears her footsteps back in the bedroom. All the while he sits in a trance, worrying the question which has distilled itself down to *What is it?*

"Come and have breakfast with me," Claire says, brushing his forehead with her lips. The flowery scent of her is one that ordinarily exhilarates Ben, but this morning it exacerbates the inner discomfort he has been feeling. He follows her into the kitchen, where the two of them move through the familiar ritual of heating muffins, pouring juice, and describing for each other what their separate days are going to be like. Claire has appointments until noon. Then she and her colleagues are having lunch together to talk about remodeling their building. She's having her hair done at two, then a couple more appointments.

Talking to Claire, listening to her, eating muffins and drinking juice with her—all these little activities make him feel better. He tells her about the project he's recently taken on, at the suggestion of the board of trustees, of going downtown to speak with the merchants who do business with the students, especially the ones who sell them alcoholic beverages. There have been some incidents lately, some bad feelings on both sides. The aim of Ben's discussions with the merchants is, of course, to locate problems and try to solve them, but it is mostly to persuade them that the college cares about the community. He expects he'll be downtown all day.

She turns her face to him. "I wonder if the college really does care about the town," she says.

Ben can see her making the effort to engage with what he's told her. He wishes her interest came naturally, but he's glad to have it anyway; willed interest, he thinks, is better than no interest at all. And he has to admit that his duties as associate dean lack a certain drama. "I sort of doubt that it does care," he says, "except that most of us who work there would like to have a nice town to live in."

"Poor Ben," Claire says. "I'm sure you care about the town. You'll do a good job talking to the merchants, I'm sure."

Ben knows he doesn't care about the town either, except for a couple of restaurants where he enjoys the food. He starts to say exactly this to Claire, because he's become impatient with the small talk. But then he decides it's just the day that has gotten him feeling cranky and wounded. Tomorrow he'll be back to his old self.

When he and Claire take their good-bye kiss, Ben doesn't settle for the usual peck-and-run. He pulls her close, he presses his cheek against her cheek, and he tells her that talking to Julie this morning reminded him all over again how grateful he is to have this life he and Claire have made for themselves. This is not exactly how he feels, but it's a feeling he aspires to have. Claire pulls away enough to look at him. For a fraction of an instant she narrows her eyes at him, as if she's reading the scroll of his consciousness for the entire morning. It's such a penetrating look that it almost shocks Ben into saying, *What?* or *God, Claire!* But then she smiles and moves back against him. "Me too," she says. Time stretches. They stand like that, holding each other in the kitchen. With Claire so solidly in his arms and the fragrance of coffee and muffins still in the air, Ben starts thinking he's going to be all right.

When she leaves, he watches her walk to her car, stash her briefcase in the backseat, then climb in the front. He watches her pull out of their driveway. At this moment he's certain he is nowhere in Claire's consciousness; her thoughts are moving ahead to what's coming to her in the next several hours. He knows that's just as it should be, but his spirits plummet anyway. A powerful urge to go back upstairs to bed comes over him. It would be something he's never done before. The idea of it makes him smile rather bitterly to himself. *Let me get through this* rises out of his consciousness.

Ben forces himself to put on his tie and jacket and to move his body out of the house and into his car. Then it is not so bad. The morning is unseasonably warm for October. He and the merchants will be able to speak cheerfully of the weather. And the way the car moves along so smoothly now pleases Ben—something he doesn't remember noticing before. If he were walking along, every step would be an act of will, but with only the slightest pressure of his foot on its accelerator, this car will take him where he needs to go. It's a miracle, really, now that he thinks about it.

As he's making the turn onto Route 7 to drive into the center of town, the sunlight across his car's hood, the particular shade of blue of the sky, the shape of a high, thick cloud, and a slow, aching swatch of the Dvořák Cello Concerto coming from the public radio station into Ben's car cause a vision of Meg at the beach at Cape May to come into his mind. He's reliving snippets of the last trip he and Julie and Meg took together. Meggie's about sixteen, a young woman but still a child, too, out there beyond the breakers, enjoying how the waves buffet her but don't knock her down. She's strong and healthy as a young horse, and she's laughing at the power of the ocean that for the moment is just kidding around with her. Ben can't keep driving, because what he can see is just too vivid. He's able to pull into a Champlain Farms parking lot, where he sits still and gives in to the very last bit of the vision, the sunlight shining across the wet skin of Meg's shoulders as she walks up out of the sea, trailing her hands in the water as she walks toward him.

That movement of the Dvořák ends. With it goes Ben's vision of Cape May. Now he feels silly sitting in his car, wiping his eyes. He puts the car back in gear and moves on into town.

When Ben turns away from plugging coins into the parking meter, he feels a set of hands take hold of his shoulders. That's when he becomes aware that he's stepped into someone's path. It's Danny Marlow, whom Ben recognizes but doesn't really know. Danny's half a head taller than Ben and at least thirty pounds heavier, most of it chest and shoulder muscles according to Ben's currently intimate perception of the man. He wouldn't have expected Danny Marlow to be as big as he apparently is—he's like a football player or a professional wrestler. Danny says, "Sorry,

Dr. McClelland, I almost ran you down there," gives Ben a faint grin as he steps to one side, then moves on down the sidewalk in the direction of Hargreaves Market.

In the warm sunlight of the morning, standing near the center of town, Ben finds himself ridiculously pleased that Danny Marlow has spoken to him by name, has even called him Doctor, though Ben hasn't encouraged anyone to call him that. He and Marlow have never been introduced, though he's been aware of the man for years. Apparently Marlow has been aware of him, too. Ben tries to imagine what sorts of things would be said about him by the people here in town. He knows he's not a particularly interesting person—the way Marlow is, for instance, with his suntan, his muscles, his mustache, and his little blue sports car. As a matter of fact, this is the first time Ben has ever thought about himself in this way, as a topic of conversation. He stands on the sidewalk, near where his car is parked, examining his pocket change as if it were the entrails of a sacrificial animal. He's completely stepped out of himself. He's imagining with remarkable clarity what Robert Hargreaves might be saying to Danny Marlow across the counter as Danny pays for a quart of orange juice—"McClelland, yeah, he's the guy who married Claire Boscowen. You remember Jim Boscowen, guy who used to raise so much hell at town meeting before they stopped letting him in? Jim Boscowen's wife divorced him some years ago. Then she married this McClelland from up at the college. She's Claire McClelland now. He's her husband."

I'm Claire's husband arrives in Ben's mind like a revelation. He pockets his change and steps toward downtown and Hargreaves Market, which is where he'd planned to make his first official visit. As he approaches the corner, the voices continue coming to him, Danny Marlow now asking, "Didn't he used to be married, too? To that lady potter who lives out on Stone's Throw Road?" and Robert Hargreaves answering, "Yes, that's right, and they had a kid, a real pretty girl who went to high school here before she went up to Middlebury."

I've stopped being Julie's husband. I'm beginning to be Claire's husband. And I'm still Meggie's dad. These pieces of who he is are falling into place in Ben's mind as he approaches the brick side of Hargreaves

Market. Of course, he knew these things before this morning, but it was as if he'd read them in a book and understood them but hadn't really absorbed them, hadn't taken them into himself. *Thank you for letting me see who I am* flies up out of the center of himself like a phrase of high notes bellowed by an operatic tenor.

The noise Ben hears to his left and behind him is the rich humming of Russian baritones, a chorus that is rather amazingly bearing down on him. He turns and meets the left fender of Margaret Allen's Buick, which is crazily moving into him right here on the sidewalk. The instant before impact, Ben crouches and turns slightly so that the point of the fender punches him in the side of his midsection, just about directly at pancreas level. Through the Buick's windshield and her thick glasses, he and Margaret look directly at each other. Then Ben feels himself flung away from the car, which continues moving obliquely down the sidewalk until it rams into the side of Hargreaves Market. Ben is sitting on his backside in the front yard of the Buddhist Meditation Center. He watches people running toward Margaret's car, which really did make a tremendous explosion when it hit the brick wall. Ben has in mind standing up and walking down that way, too—*Let me rise to this occasion* floats up through his thoughts—to see about Margaret, who is well past eighty and should have given up driving years ago. He needs to catch his breath, though. Now, while he sits here, prayers of thanks erupt out of him, one after the other, soaring into the light.

Not

My parents loved me from separate directions. My father kept his distance—his attention was of the calm and deep variety. He understood me in an almost timeless way, whereas my mother discerned my immediate mood, my latest whim, my shifting tastes in clothes, hair, boys, food, and music. Until recently I didn't think all that much about my parents. Or when I thought about them, it was in a nostalgic haze—they were remarkable, my childhood was a blessing, and so on. Now, nearing forty, when I've had to reconsider everything, I've become skeptical. Maybe all that love and attention I received as a child damaged me. Or maybe it was my parents' deaths that did it. At any rate, I'm not going to be able to go on with the life I have so carefully constructed for myself here in town.

· ——— ·

Wherever I turned, I faced darker and darker corridors. Then it occurred to me: more than anyone I know, I have a choice. Now there is this distant light, as if I am soon to be released into a meadow of sunlit green.

· ——— ·

Candles
Coleman lantern
Sleeping bag
Portable cookstove

. ——— .

There was an intensity to the way my mother waited for me to come home from school. At first she was waiting for me right outside the door of my kindergarten classroom. One afternoon of my sophomore year in high school I told her, "God, Mom, you've got all your lights on. Can't you just cool it?" She was amused by that, as I knew she would be. We both knew she wasn't going to change her ways. To tell the truth, I was rarely so happy as when I was a teenager walking home from school knowing I would be grandly received by my mother. When I came in through the kitchen door, my favorite snack was waiting for me on the table, the milk freshly poured into its glass, the Rice Krispie cakes still warm from the oven. My mother's whole body was alert for my arrival, her eyes beaming in on me. In her last days at home, she was slumped in her rocking chair at our kitchen window, blinking and heavily medicated for pain, but nevertheless focused and waiting for me to enter her field of vision.

. ——— .

Though not in any hurry, I've begun to pack. For outdoor clothing, I own only the odd shirt, pair of boots, and slacks—so I'm shopping. L. L. Bean and Eddie Bauer have become significant. Cotton underwear has become significant.

. ——— .

I live alone.
I have money.
I know the right place.

. ——— .

Easy enough to pay bills, examine my accounts, take inventory, and so on. I've discovered that I'm actually "worth" more than I ever imagined possible for someone like me. But I also want as much cash as I can conveniently carry, at the same time I want not to attract the attention of the bankers, brokers, and clerks who keep track of my assets. For example, the money due me from Ben's retirement fund can't be touched without making it evident that I'm making a change in my life. So I'll let that money go. I'll also let go a couple of insurance policies, substantial assets that will simply disappear when my payments stop coming in. Now that I realize how much money I can actually get my hands on, I see that I'm not really "worth" very much at all. That's reassuring.

. ——— .

Solitude and time.
I must not be interfered with.

. ——— .

To trade cars, yesterday I drove up to the Jeep dealer in Rutland. No one there knows anything about me. When I asked for a woman salesperson, they granted me Jody Gonyaw in a khaki skirt and a sky-blue cable-knit sweater that brought out the blue of her eyes. With Jody I took my time looking at four-wheel-drive vehicles. We seemed to have a lot to say to each other; she had kids and a husband to tell me about, and I had questions to ask her. About myself I was careful to tell her very little. When I finally picked out the black Cherokee I wanted, she and I agreed on the terms of my trade-in. Then we discussed the best date to carry out the transaction. I've decided to pack up everything from home, lock the house, drive to Rutland, transfer all my gear into the new vehicle, and keep driving north. May 22nd, that's my date. Ha! When I said good-bye to Jody—she'd walked me out to my car—I sensed she was about to give me a hug, the way people in a family do. I wanted exactly that—and so stepped toward her. Then we both seemed to catch ourselves. We shook hands. When I was in my car, starting it and watching her walk back inside the showroom, her skirt fluttering a little with the breeze, I felt my eyes stinging.

. ——— .

Seeds and a set of small gardening tools. If there is to be a garden at all, it will have to be a plot not much larger than my coffee table. As if for a child. Most likely there will be no garden at all. I can't imagine there will be an open piece of ground. I can't imagine I will want to do the work of it. Still, it may give me something to help pass the time.

. ——— .

I want to confide in Jody Gonyaw. To call her up and tell her everything.

. ——— .

There are of course my clients. When I consider what to do about them, I can't avoid seeing that more and more, as the years have gone by, these people have been consuming my life. From this perspective—a perspective I've never achieved from my individual dealings with them—I've become detached from the entire lot. To certain ones I want to dash off notes: *Dear Charles Patterson, forget about leaving your wife and children, you lack sufficient gumption to be on your own. Dear Mrs. Leverett, yes, please do put your mother in a nursing home, you're right, it will be the best for all concerned—your children will be grateful. Dear Sally Quarles, if you don't break it off with that deadbeat chiropractor, you're a bigger fool than he is (which is saying something).* And so on. Ones who have wrung my heart with their sorrows now seem to me whiners, slackers, emotional cowards, spoiled children. I'm horrified that I've lost my compassion. But I'm even more horrified at the sight of my clients in this cold light. After spending hundreds of hours discussing the most basic issues with these people, I see that I might just as well have said, *Grow up! Take responsibility! Learn to fend for yourself!* They've wasted my time. Or I've wasted theirs.

. ——— .

State-of-the-art sleeping bag

·———·

I want to have a talk with Jim. As I've made my preparations, this is the oddest thing that has come over me—a need or a desire, I don't know which. I don't even know what topic I want to take up with him. At any rate, it's impossible. After the first year or so of our marriage, there weren't any decent talks to be had with Jim. And these days he has, as lay people say, lost his mind.

·———·

Bug repellent
Toilet paper
Rain gear
Cotton underwear

·———·

A client of mine—I will call him Robert—had been thinking of running his car, at high speed, into a tree or a bridge or a rock wall on the interstate. He hadn't yet felt desperate, but he imagined he might one day or night feel forlorn enough that he would need to know the right place to go to end his life. So for years, in this casual way, Robert kept his eye out for good trees, good rocks, and so on. A girlfriend of Robert's had once, in the early hours of a morning, tried to make herself run into those enormous stone cliffs and pillars they've left in the median of Interstate 89. She hadn't succeeded. She would swerve her car off the road and aim it toward a cliff face, then chicken out and swerve the car back onto the highway. She hadn't the nerve to hold the car on course for her target. She drove almost to Canada before she gave up. Robert thought it was because she hadn't been selective, hadn't picked the right target and focused her concentration. So he was on the lookout for just the right immovable object. Certain trees on certain highways were attractive to him, but he worried that he, too, would chicken out and swerve away. He foresaw humiliating scenes of having to explain why, when he wasn't drunk, his car had plunged a hundred yards out into a farmer's field. He needed a target that really wouldn't let him change his mind once he'd begun his charge. Driving down the mountain on Route 9 toward Wilmington one day, he found a boulder placed just at the deepest point of a sharp curve. Before that curve there was a straight stretch of road that would let a car reach a speed of 75 or 85 m.p.h. Once you were going that fast, you'd never make the curve anyway, even if you changed your mind. And you could start building your speed before you ever saw the boulder. It was a discrete rock, round and smoothed as an elephant's back and about the size of a house trailer, light gray in color. The rock was even slightly shielded by a scrubby little tree and some high grass. Robert said knowing that he had picked it out of the landscape pleased him, as if it were a secret discovery he had made, as if no one else could know about that rock. And certainly—until he told me—no one knew what the rock meant to him. Robert said that after he found that rock, he went out of his way to drive by it. He expected he would go on needing to see it. After he found the right rock, Robert's life changed. For the better. Decidedly for the better, he said.

· ⸺ ·

Small fishing rod
Fishing tackle
Books on fishing
Field guides

· ⸺ ·

Today I drove past a man pushing a grocery cart full of bottles right down the middle of McKenzie Street—a man in a tweed jacket, a white shirt, and a tie! His pace and posture signified to the world that he and his bottles were as entitled to their part of the street as any Saab-driving student. His walk was familiar to me.

A full half minute after I had lost sight of the man, I realized that for almost ten years I had lived with him. It was Jim. Then this additional thought came: *I understand Jim now. I know why he has chosen this life. So I am the only person who knows him.* My reflective haze was so intense that I drove several blocks before I felt the shock of the question that had taken its time getting to me: *Who knows me?*

· —— ·

Detergent
Teakettle
Pot
Skillet

· —— ·

Another sensation comes when I wake up in the middle of the night: drifting outward in space, away from my home planet, as if, as in a movie or book, I have been dispatched on a mission but somehow—once out here, far too far out ever to be able to get back alone—cut loose and abandoned. Thus my fate is to spin and drift out here in my space suit in the cold darkness punctuated only by distant stars and to call out, *Claire to Earth. Claire to Anybody. Come in please.* When I stand up from bed to go for a drink of water, I am dizzy.

· —— ·

What to take to read? Not what I have loved—Jane Austen, Flaubert, Tolstoy. But what I thought I would eventually get around to reading. The complete works of Freud. Proust. George Eliot. One of those. I'll need a few books to read but not so many.

· —— ·

Do I want to smell as I have smelled all these civilized years of my life, or do I want to smell like myself? Ah, the question of deodorant: what an idiocy.

· —— ·

A handgun

. ——— .

Not necessary to communicate with Danny. He comes to mind as I need him—nightly—but it is not necessary to communicate with him. Danny can think whatever he wishes to think.

. ——— .

Kleenex
Matches
A small shovel

. ——— .

To be a displaced person in the midst of what is ordinarily thought to be a rich life. Without meaning to, without realizing when it occurs, somewhere in the past, you make a wrong step. Maybe it happens when you're four or five years old. You can't realize the implications of the next ten minutes, let alone the rest of your life. You climb a tree and hide from Polly, your best friend. You don't answer when Polly calls out to you, a small personal infraction, something you think is just very interesting, and maybe a little mean. But when you do it, your life turns ever so slightly the wrong way, a turn that twenty years later will make a huge difference, but of course you can't realize that at the time. There must be many people who never have the misfortune to discover their displacement. Danny, too, is a displaced one, but he probably knows. If I had ever explained it to him, he would have nodded in that thickheaded way of his. "Yep," he would say—and make that smug downward jerk of his chin. Damn him!

. ——— .

Toothpaste
Toothbrush

Hairbrush
Deodorant. All right, deodorant. What about a mirror?

. ——— .

No.

. ——— .

To envision another life. Before each of my marriages and also before my divorce from Jim, I did this—made up how my new life was going to be. Imagination scouts out ahead. One hopes to conquer the strangeness of the future. One tries to persuade oneself to be less afraid.

. ——— .

Sewing kit
Heavy scissors

. ——— .

What is this stupid desire to reveal my innermost self to inappropriate people? Jody Gonyaw could do little more than pat me on the shoulder. Jim could snarl at me. I need a good therapist!

. ——— .

My Grandfather Thompson came to possess an obscure plot of land—what had been, or what had tried to be, around the turn of the century a hillside farm—several miles south of Lincoln. When I was eighteen, my father took me to it. We needed a map, a compass, and most of a day to hike in to it. There was a stone fence; otherwise, it had grown up so badly we wouldn't have known we were there. But we found a logging trail that went along beside the property and that had been partially maintained. We marked that trail on the map, and I have the map in my safety deposit box.

There was a spring, too, though the springhouse had long ago collapsed and rotted away. We found what my father told me they used to call a dairy, a cavelike structure where they stored potatoes and apples, things that could be preserved for months if they were kept dry and cool. For being made mostly of stone and earth anyway, the dairy was intact. Even its oversized heavy wooden door had stayed dry enough not to have rotted. Inside it, my father and I stood some moments, letting our eyes adjust to the darkness. It was cool in there. There were shelves along the walls, and some shapes were on those shelves, but without a flashlight neither my father nor I wanted to explore. Spiders were likely we said. We said we would remember to bring a light the next time we came. But such a smell that underground room had!—like a plowed field on a rainy night. I am remembering it because we seemed to have penetrated into its essence. It is to that fragrance I mean to return.

· ——— ·

When Ben was killed, I took none of the sleeping medication Dick Haller prescribed and picked up and brought over for me. Halcion. I kept it. I have it.

· ——— ·

Flashlight

· ——— ·

My Grandfather Thompson was a grocer in Burlington who extended credit to his customers. The deed and the map to the Lincoln farm came to him in payment of a debt. He never saw the place, never set a foot onto the property. When he died, the deed and the map came to my father. When my father died, the deed and the map came to me. On the map it is called Cobb Hill Farm. I own it.

· ——— ·

Notebooks
Pens

. ——— .

Only after I had built up my practice, only after I began hearing the stories of many other people, did I realize how lonely it is
for me to be without family. Even Danny, Mr. Alone himself, has
his mother here in town and brothers and a sister. My mother died
when I was still in high school; my father died a dozen years ago.
There is a great-aunt in a nursing home in Boston, and there are
some distant cousins scattered across the country, no one I am in
touch with. No one. But what difference would family make now?
I've been without anybody for too long. I can't imagine it anymore, can't imagine having my mother alive. To be able to talk to
my mother?! The idea makes my teeth chatter.

. ——— .

An excellent battery-powered clock.
A battery for my wristwatch. (Ask the guy at Time Flies to
show me how to change it myself.)

. ——— .

Long before daylight, I'm awake. All my things are set out to
be packed in a suitcase or box. Everything fits because I have already tried it all, already worked out the arrangement of each item
in its container. I've parked in the driveway so that the streetlight
will shine on the car trunk and I won't have to turn on the outside lights to see. I know where each piece goes in the car, anyway. That, too, I worked out earlier. In their immense effort to
go unnoticed, this is how commandos and spies perform: plans
rehearsed sufficiently to make thought unnecessary.

. ——— .

A cool, damp morning.
A clear sky in every direction.

. —— .

Driving up Route 7 just at sunup is enough to make me change my mind. A sky that reminds me of mornings in my childhood, green valley land and mountains, cows and the smell of the Vermont springtime—which is to say the smell of cow manure. On such a morning, what could possibly stand between me and my life? Even now, it's not too late. I could call my morning clients and cancel—it's Monday, and I remember who they are and the times of their appointments. I could trade cars, unpack this old one and repack my new one just as I've planned. But then drive back to Bennington. Drive back to the office in time to meet my afternoon appointments.

. —— .

I know what stands between me and my life. My life.

. —— .

Breakfast at the Sewards Family Diner in Rutland, where years ago I came with my father for doughnuts and ice cream. This morning I take a booth by myself and set my elbows on the indestructible formica table alongside the indestructible salt, pepper, and sugar containers. According to the menu, I can still order doughnuts and ice cream. For years now, my breakfast has been a banana, a glass of orange juice, a vitamin pill, and strong black coffee. The waitress is older than I am, a cheerful woman in a clean white uniform. I am free to order whatever I want. When I look at her, she smiles. Does she recognize me? Of course not. But she could have been here when I walked in with my father twenty years ago. "What'll you have, honey?" "I'll take the glazed doughnuts and vanilla ice cream, please." "Coffee?" "Yes, please." "Cream?" "No, thank you." And of course as she's walking back up the aisle I want to tell her what I'm up to today. "How would you like to hear a story?" I could say. I'm pathological, there's no doubt about it. If I knew her well—if she were my lover, for instance—I'd be doing everything I could to keep her from finding out what I'm up to.

·———·

In the parking lot of Sewards, the morning has warmed enough for me to take off my sweater before I get back in my car. I've always liked the sun on my arms—the sun in springtime, when it reminds me there are warm, comfortable days ahead.

·———·

A full tank of gas in Ripton.

No. Before I turn off Route 7, a station too busy for me to be noticed or remembered.

·———·

Jody Gonyaw is not at the Jeep dealer's. I realize I half expected her to be standing out in the parking lot waiting for me to pull in this morning. Ed Irwin, the sales manager, explains to me that Jody has called in sick today and that she's asked him to handle the paperwork. All right, I say, but now I'm hating this occasion that I'd been looking forward to. It doesn't take long. Ed isn't looking for small talk, and I'm brooding. I sign documents where he tells me to. I hand him the certified check for the exact amount. It is the check that will close my account in Bennington, but Ed doesn't know that and wouldn't care if he did know it. I had anticipated handing this check to Jody as a delicious moment, though, she, too, wouldn't have been able to appreciate how neatly and invisibly this transaction is closing my old life. I had even imagined the look on my face when I handed her the check and the look on her face when she took it from me. There's no look whatsoever on Ed's face. He asks me to wait while he changes the license plates from my old car to my new Jeep. I don't know why he doesn't want me to watch, but I also don't mind waiting in his little cubicle of an office with all his pitiful little salesman-of-the-month plaques on the wall. I counsel myself against feeling this sadness at Jody's not being here. But I can't help it. I am on the verge of tears. When Ed comes back, I ask him to wait while I transfer my things. "It's only fair," I tell him when he offers to help. "You didn't want me to help you. Now I don't want you to help me. Just stay put until I bring you the keys. Okay?" I make him agree. Then, outside in the sunlight, I find that the day is already too hot, and I am too upset to avoid making a public display in a parking lot; I furiously slam crates, packs, and boxes into the back of my new Jeep. This is what my life has come to! I am just so deeply angry.

. —— .

An ax. A long-handled ax—the kind that will let you chop your foot off if that's what you're in the mood to do! I'll take a chance and stop at one of these country hardware stores along Route 7 and buy just such an ax. That way if they do track me down, at least I'll be remembered as the lady who bought the ax.

. —— .

Hot now. On the radio, the weather report says it's going to be hot all day. Tonight, though, when I am in the mountains, I am certain it will be cool.

. —— .

In the middle of Brandon, Vermont, at 11:30 A.M., at the sharp curve of Route 7 where the ramshackle Brandon Inn sits, a contrary theory of human relations settles over my mind: *wrong partners*. The books say we always choose an equal, but the books are wrong. Asymmetry is the biological principle: we look for the one who's more powerful or less powerful, smarter or less smart, more beautiful or less, whatever, just so it isn't equal. Never look for equal. Equals push away from each other. The only reason I could marry Jim and then Ben was that the balance was in my favor. Jim wasn't as smart, Ben didn't have as much energy. So does that explain why I can't care about Danny? Because it might be equal with him? In all this sunlight, with all these things to see on both sides of the highway, why is this worn-out topic the one I'm stuck thinking about? Whether or not "wrong partners" is an accurate theory, I don't want Danny. I just don't want him. I don't want. I don't. And what theory is it that accounts for this black hole that has opened up in me in the approximate vicinity of where there's supposed to be a soul? I'm not required to love Danny Marlow—he didn't ask that. It's only required that I be able to love. Somebody. Anybody. Anything. And I don't. Haven't. Won't. Can't.

· ——— ·

In the Help Business, I was a fraud. I had no business trying to help anyone.

· ——— ·

The consolations of a new car. If it's true that there aren't atheists in foxholes, it's probably also true that there aren't any truly reflective people behind the wheel of a new Jeep Cherokee. Maybe I should find myself an interstate and put this lovely machine on the open road until it's an old car instead of a new one. I've got a box full of cash with me; I could certainly keep going for a while. But I know where I have to go, I know what I have to do, and it doesn't require an interstate. It means turning up Route 125 right here. I haven't driven through East Middlebury since my father and I made that trip all those years ago. So far as I can tell, East Middlebury hasn't changed. The world evolves into technological chaos, my father goes to his grave, I grow up and wear myself out, but East Middlebury remains the same.

· ——— ·

Stop for gas at the blinking light. A mom-and-pop, but a busy one. They won't notice me.

· ——— ·

I doubted my mother's devotion to my father. Or rather I doubted its authenticity. Her attentions to him were out of a story-book. It was as if she felt she had to demonstrate wifely devotion to him, to me, to their friends, to anyone who knew them or saw them together. I think my father had his doubts, too, though I never heard him express them. When he came home from work, she had a little snack waiting for him on a tray. While he washed his hands at the kitchen sink, she told him what she was fixing for supper. She asked him questions about his day at work. Then when he was ready to sit down with the newspaper, she took a can of Miller High Life from the refrigerator and my father's beer mug from the freezer. These she set on the tray with his snack—usually crackers and cheese but sometimes one of those single-serving glass cups of shrimp and cocktail sauce she had bought from the grocery store. Following him into the living room, she carried the tray to the end table beside his chair, the chair where she always made certain the newspaper waited for him. She stood and watched while he opened and poured the beer. Then she carried the empty can back to the kitchen. As she walked away from him, my father seemed to be studying her back. Sometimes he shook his head and smiled at her retreating figure—but whether out of affection or astonishment I wasn't able to discern. Some of each, I supposed. For many years they did this every day. I had the sense of my father's being uncomfortable with the ritual and my mother's carrying it out relentlessly, as if someone had driven home to her a lesson on the correct procedure for welcoming a husband back to the household after his day of work. Of course her own mother must have somehow trained her to be that kind of wife. And she in turn, without thinking about it, was training me to be that kind of wife. I wondered what lay on the other side of that carefully constructed devotion. Even as a child, I wondered what my mother's true feelings were for my father. Maybe I even wondered what my true feelings would be for the husband who was waiting for me out in the future. It was pretty obvious that the endpoint of all of that demonstration must have been the elimination of true feelings. And I was right. She was showing me that that was how you did it, you used the ritual to get rid of the feelings. For a while I even worried that that was what Ben was up to by bringing me coffee every morning. He wasn't—Ben was a naturally affectionate person—but he might have agreed with my mother that a ritual like that was what you needed to stay married. My mother of course died before she had been married twenty years. But even if she'd lived to be married fifty or sixty years, she'd have gone on just that way.

. ——— .

The smell of a Vermont mom-and-pop with a wooden floor: candy/meat/cheese/kerosene/bubblegum. They ought to market it as a fragrance in New York. I can't resist a couple of red Twizzlers.

. ——— .

Was she ever false with me? When she was alive, I never doubted her. When I looked at my mother's face, I took it for granted her feelings for me were absolute. I thought she was beaming toward me exactly what my father would never receive from her—the pure adoration that was mine and mine alone. But there must have been a slight disturbance in that signal, because after she died, I began to doubt her. I think she was struggling to feel what she thought she should feel for me. I think the poor woman must have been like me.

. ——— .

The bridge at the uphill side of East Middlebury lies directly on a sharp curve. It was here that my father said a thing that comes back to me now: "This is the end of civilization for a while, my

dear. It's another world up here." When we started up the mountain, it was clear what he meant. Today it is also clear what he
meant. The mountain is so steep, the rocks and woods so present
out there, that I realize how little the natural world is part of my
ordinary life. I catch a glimpse of how much a part of my life the
natural world is about to be. The cool scent of trees and water flies
in my windows. This is what I want.

· —— ·

Ben told me that his daughter, Meghan, once cursed at the
birds outside her window. It was an early summer morning, her
windows were open, she had gone to bed late, she was thirteen
and having trouble sleeping anyway because of her braces and
headgear, and the birds made a racket that would have woken
an Egyptian mummy. Meghan sat up in bed and screamed out her
window, "Shut the fuck up!" Ben said he worried about her doing
that. He sympathized with her but thought you shouldn't curse at
the birds. He could never think of a way to bring it up to discuss
with her, though. Meghan seemed to be able to go back to sleep
right away, and Ben didn't even know if she remembered what she
had done. She did it only that once.

· —— ·

The mountain barely tolerates the road. It makes the road
squirm. If it wished, the mountain could heave this asphalt scab off
its skin. If people still wanted to drive cars up its side, they would
have to start over again, they would have to build another road.

· —— ·

Where the sun strikes the road, it feels hot in my car. Then I
pass underneath the trees into a shady stretch, and it's immediately
cool enough to bring bumps to my arm. I've thought of winter, of
course, but this is the first time I've been able to imagine how it
might be. If I get that far, I'll have to drive out and buy a load of

supplies. I'll need to teach myself how to walk on snowshoes. Did I ever do that when I was a kid? Did my father try to teach me? At any rate, I can't imagine I'll get that far.

. ——— .

Parka
Long underwear
Heavy gloves
Hat

. ——— .

The Ripton Country Store is tempting—a red building whose porch hangs over onto the shoulder of Route 125. But if I set a foot in there today, they may remember me if the police come asking. Still, to know that it's here is reassuring. If I had to, I could probably walk this far.

. ——— .

I used to think a lot about how it would have been if I'd never married Jim Boscowen and had instead married Ben McClelland when I was twenty—except it would have had to be when I was twenty-one or -two, because Ben would have wanted me to graduate from UVM first. Ben and I came to sex in our middle age, and yes, sure, I was disappointed—he was, too, though neither of us said so. If we'd been younger, I'm sure it would have been different. I'd give a lot not to have had to witness how Jim turned cruel and not to have experienced the cruel things he did. All my good memories of Jim can't make up for the bad. But Ben was a healing force. I knew he'd always try to be good to me. When Ben was alive, I thought our days together would just go on and on, and they would be days of sweet ordinariness. That was a future I could live with.

. ——— .

I'm going back to a home I never had.

. ——— .

Those years ago when my father took me up here, Lincoln Road wasn't marked. When we took the left-hand turn off of 125, he said that Lincoln Road was what it was called but that it would never be marked. People up here just knew the road or else they had no business turning onto it. Well, it's marked now. My father wasn't right about everything. Or maybe it was just the way he wanted me to think about things up here in the mountains—that different world he wanted me to witness before I went off to college. At any rate, it's still a dirt road.

. ——— .

I did occasionally imagine marrying Danny. That is, I imagined the ceremony. A justice of the peace in some faraway place is probably how we would have done it if he had talked me into it. But in my imagination I always saw our wedding at the First Congo Church right in the center of town, Danny swelling his chest up in a ruffled shirt and a white dinner jacket. I saw it with everybody there we know. My cheeks got hot when the images played across my mind. Just imagining that wedding I got so embarrassed I found myself chuckling aloud. It would almost have been worth doing just to see how my friends behaved when they went through the reception line. Danny would have been so pleased with himself I'd have had to elbow him in the ribs.

. ——— .

I bear right and pass under a stretch of trees on both sides of the road, a swooping aisle of shade splotched with sunlight. Slowly, slowly, that's how I drive this Jeep—so slowly that I make no dust. I wish I could make this part of the trip last for hours.

. ——— .

The question of fuel for the winter. Ah, that knotty question. I want to live my days up here without thinking of exactly this kind of question. But if I don't think of it, if I don't make a project out of it while the weather is warm, the question will be quite easily resolved, because there will be no fuel for the winter.

·————·

After the bridge across Alder Brook, I slow to a stop and set the Jeep into four-wheel drive. Then I start up again, looking for the logging trail off to the right.

·————·

When I was around eight years old and asked my father what he was afraid of as a kid, he confessed to me he was still afraid of the dark. "I've never been terrified of it," he said, "but the only time I like it is when I'm in bed about to go to sleep." As confessions go, his was a small one, but to me it seemed shameful. I never told anyone else this secret.

·————·

What I want more than anything—maybe because I've never done it: to be still on a sunny day. To spend hours watching the wind stir the leaves on the trees.

·————·

The trail is here, clear enough for me to see only because I am looking for it. When I turn, I feel as if I am pushing myself into these woods, willfully inserting myself. My Cherokee is committing a violation, shrubs and tree limbs very nearly block my vision but fall away to the side as I press on. Then the way opens up, the trail becomes much more clear. I can see ahead. The woods seem to be telling me, *Oh well, now that you're here, come on in. This way, please.* The air feels wet and smells like creek-bank ferns.

·————·

Why did my father want to show me this world up here?
And why does this question suddenly plunk itself onto the hood
of my Jeep to stare in at me through the windshield? When he and
I came up here to try to locate the old Cobb Hill Farm, I had just
graduated from high school. At the time I never questioned his
motives. We discussed it, we planned it, but it was essentially just a
trip we were taking together. Only now does it occur to me that it
was the only trip like this we ever took—exploring the wilderness, really a kind of adventure. Though he never expressed it
himself, I seemed to know what he had in mind, didn't I? So what
was it? My mother had been dead long enough for the grieving to
have lessened. My father and I could be cheerful around each
other again, without faking it as we had done for so many months.
I'd even begun going out with boys again, having stopped dating
completely the year before she died, when I understood how truly
ill she was. Though Jim Boscowen had managed to keep himself
constantly present in my life anyway. He would appear at the door
with some little gift he said his mother was sending us, a box
of cookies, a little bouquet of garden flowers, certainly things he
could have gotten himself and brought to our door. I suspected
that Jim was fabricating his mother's concern for us, because we
hardly knew the Boscowens. I appreciated such deviousness on his
part, as well as the fact that he sometimes showed up wearing a
tie. But when my father came to the door, Jim engaged him in
such earnest conversation that my father came back indoors shak-
ing his head. So there was that resistance on my father's part.
Maybe I understood that my father was giving me a little time
away from Jim Boscowen's persistent attention.

· —— ·

A wall of vegetation: the trail simply ends. I stop the Jeep to
step out and see how much cutting I'll have to do to be able to
turn around. I must have taken the wrong turn off the dirt road.
Even when I step up to the barrier of leaves and branches, it appears impenetrable. But I step directly into it, pushing branches
aside. And step farther still. The limbs give and let me penetrate. In

five steps I have moved through the wall into a clear trail again. Here the woods have turned to pine and spruce. The smell is brisker, sharper; the air is warm and richly ozone scented. Green light seems caught beneath the trees—there's an airy space on both sides of the trail and up ahead. I step back to the Jeep, start it up, and drive straight through the odd little barrier. Proceeding, I feel absurdly victorious, as if I've defeated some highly intelligent opponent.

. ——— .

There was a conversation my father initiated that was deceptively casual. After we made our way out of the woods, it was nearly dark, and we were very tired. So we spent that night at the Inn, across the road from the Ripton Country Store. After our day of exploration, the Inn's country-style dinner tasted glorious. Over dessert, my father cleared his throat and then started a conversation that seemed to be over before it had begun. More than what he said, I recall the tension in his face. At first I was uneasy about what he wanted to discuss. Then I was relieved that it was something so inconsequential and that we finished the discussion so quickly. But what was it, what topic was it that he brought up into those mountains to discuss with me? Was making the occasion for that conversation the main reason for the journey? The only reason? "Claire," he began. I remember that much. That he sounded my name like that, at the beginning of what he was going to say, always meant something serious was on his mind.

. ——— .

At this fork I could go off to the right, where the trail seems clearest, or I could keep going straight ahead. So I have to stop and study the map with a magnifying glass. It's just after 2:30 in the afternoon. Tonight I can sleep in the Jeep, of course, but it's a matter of some urgency with me to find the farm before it gets dark. If I have to spend the night out here in these woods without having found it, I'll feel desperate. Dislocated. I know this is all in my mind. One place out here is the same as another. Legally, the farm belongs to me, of course, but it's just a chunk of this mountain that isn't much different from the chunk where I'm sitting right now in my idling Jeep. The map won't answer my question of direction. On the logging road I'm supposed to be on, there's no fork. There is a bend to the right that could be the turn I see directly in front of me. At any rate, my instinct is to go right.

. ——— .

The Jeep leaves its tracks. I can find my way out.

. ——— .

"Claire," he began. "Claire, your mother . . ." All right. Something to do with my mother. Something he was about to tell me about my mother. "Claire, your mother . . ." Would want? Would have wanted? He was about to tell me something my mother had in mind for me. Or wanted me to do. What?

. ——— .

I remember this tiny brook, the way it dashes down from those mossy rocks. The trail crosses directly over it—or through it. I drive slowly across the stream before stopping the Jeep, switching it off, and stepping out. Twenty years ago my father and I set down our packs and knelt here, cupped our hands and drank this water. Now I do the same. Then I use both hands to splash its iciness onto my face. I really am here. I am absolutely here. I rise, stand still, and let the breeze cool my wet face and hands. Soughing in the wind like this, the pines all around and above me are lonely and mournful. Don't be sad, I want to tell them. I'm joking, because I really don't mind at all if they're sad. Then I want to hear my voice say it. I release the words, *Don't be sad*. I utter the three sounds, but the silence whisks them away. Having spoken aloud into the wilderness, standing here in the flickering light, I feel strange. My Jeep might have understood me, but I doubt it. It ticks in the cooling air. *Come on*, it tells me. *Let's get a move on.*

. ——— .

No. It wasn't that my mother wanted something for me or wanted me to do something. My father's actual words, enunciated with some care across the square of white tablecloth, were, "Claire, your mother might have had a better life." And what I replied—without giving it the slightest bit of thought—was, "I know that, Dad." My mother's chosen martyrdom seemed to me perfectly obvious. My father sat quietly then, searching my face in the candlelight of the dining room of the Chipman Inn. "Do you, darling?" he said. He sounded disappointed but nevertheless affectionate and wistful. And that was it for that conversation. Soon, we rose from the table and went upstairs to our separate rooms. I wondered vaguely why he had made such a big production in order to say something so obvious, but I was too quickly and too deeply asleep that night to give it much thought. Right now, with my Jeep swaying up this rocky hillside like a rowboat in a hurricane, I'm realizing that my father meant to tell me something that wasn't obvious at all. He had something to tell me about my mother. I feel awful that I didn't ask him what he meant or just keep my mouth shut and let him go on. He must have gone to his grave feeling he should have told me whatever it was.

. ——— .

A client I will call Robin described her extreme depression to me as "the bottom dropping out." She was comfortably married, but she and her husband had had three children, one immediately after the other, before Robin realized that maybe she wasn't, as she put it, "cut out to be a mom." She had been seeing me for more than a year, but on this particular morning she asked to be referred to someone with a medical degree who could prescribe an anti-depressant for her. "I've been depressed before, Claire, you know that. But this makes that depression look like the Christmas spirit. This makes me wonder why I've put up with this shit all these years. I have to feel better than this, or else I'm checking out." Her voice was so feisty and definite that I found it hard to believe she felt as bad as she said she did. Nevertheless, I gave her the referral to Dick Haller, who saw her that afternoon and immediately prescribed Prozac. The literature says that Prozac has no discernible effect on the personality of the patient, but I beg to differ. Before Robin began taking it, I always liked her; she had a funny way of telling me about her latest episodes of maternal incompetence. I was convinced she was a much more responsible mother than she portrayed herself as being. After she started taking Prozac, however, she took on an attitude of indifference that worried me. One morning I told her that I missed her sense of humor. She laughed then, with an edge to her voice, and said, "Yeah, I know what you mean, Claire. I live in Whatever City nowadays. It ain't great, but it beats the hell out of where I lived before I went on this stuff." Other clients I've had who took the new antidepressants were less noticeably affected by them, although no client I've ever seen has made me think well of those drugs. With Robin, though, I was always tempted to say, "You know, Robin, I think we should discuss some other options."

·———·

The stone fence is still here!

·———·

Before he retired, my father was superintendent of schools for the Greater Bennington district. But when I was in grade school, he was the assistant superintendent for Addison County, and we lived in Middlebury. That's how he knew how it is up here where Cobb Hill Farm is located. He was bemused by the people who live in Vermont mountain communities like Ripton and Lincoln— but bemused in a respectful way. Driving back from our trip, he said, "Those Potvins and Lesperances and Dragons! I'll tell you, it

takes more backbone than most people have just to live through
a winter up there, not to mention thriving the way they do. Intelligence, too," he said. "It takes that." Then he laughed and added,
"But not the kind of intelligence you and I are used to seeing."

. ——— .

Robin's phrase *checking out*: as in checking out of a motel.
Moving on.

. ——— .

Something is different. I've definitely reached the old Cobb
Hill Farm—the way the air smells tells me that much—but it's as
if I've made a different approach to it. Or maybe I just haven't
remembered exactly how my father and I entered the property. I
leave the Jeep and follow the fence line. The stacked-up stones are
visible, but the fallen or knocked-over ones are not so visible. As I
make my way, with my boots I seem to be able to feel them out
among the vines and weeds. Then, all of a sudden, I am staring at
the flat surface of a cream-colored stone speckled with gray and
inscribed with lines of words and numbers.

. ——— .

That last afternoon I saw Danny, I could hardly make myself
speak to him, let alone look directly at him. I had to force myself
to meet his eye even for a moment. But I remember it as a normal
working day until the hour before he came. Then a cancellation left
that hour free. Ordinarily, I enjoyed having time to myself before Danny arrived. Usually, I tended my plants and thought about
how we were going to be with each other in just a short time. Our
first morning, lying on the floor after we'd so shockingly just gone
at each other, when we were both looking for something to say,
Danny said that the minute he had walked into my office and saw
my little rain forest over by the windows, he knew he had a hot
ticket on his hands. I took it as teasing and chose to laugh. I said I

liked that term, "hot ticket." The fact that Danny never said anything so witty again has made me understand that he has no sense
of humor and that he wasn't teasing.

At any rate, in my free hour my plants were reminding me of
that first morning with him, and I was wishing Danny could have
let it alone, could have just come to me once or twice a week and
taken his pleasure and then gone about his business. I would have
been happy enough to remain his "hot ticket." I had all this affection for Danny's body. He thought it was because of his muscles
and all that bulk and tautness he had worked so hard to attain, but
what I actually liked was his thickness, his height, his weight. He
was as big as Jim Boscowen and Ben McClelland put together. And
I liked how delicately he moved. I liked his hands and his feet—his
ears and even the nape of his neck. The pure truth of it is that I
liked the way Danny's body understood my body. Sex with Jim and
Ben had been like trying to dance with someone clumsy—you can
get through the experience, but it isn't dancing, and it isn't something you're eager to repeat. Sex with Danny was the way I
imagine dancing with Gene Kelly or Fred Astaire would be. His
body's slightest movement was exactly right. His timing was my
timing. If my body wanted or needed something, his body discerned it and gave it. Would that Danny himself had the subtlety
and intelligence of his body. I struggled to like Danny, or at least to
stop disliking him. It hurt me to want a person I didn't enjoy for
any other reason than sex. I began to think I was in worse shape
than most of my clients. By that last afternoon, I was at a point
where just hearing him speak was more than I could bear. When
he was talking to me, "Please just shut up and fuck me" was on
the tip of my tongue.

· ——— ·

Benjamin Scully
1846–1898
That He Struggled
Not In Vain

· ——— ·

From the beginning I was ashamed of how I felt about Danny Marlow. I had to do something.

. ——— .

I have, so to speak, stumbled into the family graveyard of Cobb Hill Farm. Edward Scully was the man who deeded the property over to my grandfather—Edward Scully was almost certainly the son of this Benjamin Scully whose bones are buried here. The small square of these stone walls becomes visible to me now that I know to look for it. So I go kicking through the vines and leaves. At least five more gravestones are here, along with some stones that must be markers for infants or small children. I find myself looking up through the beech and maple leaves to the cloudless sky. Here in these mountains, families lived and died, birthed and buried each other; they might as well have been in outer space. Their lifetimes passed unremarked. Edward Scully moved down out of the mountain to enter the larger world, and look what happened to him. He lost his inheritance. I have moved up to his green, airy land to claim my inheritance. What will happen to me? Tweet and twitter of birdsong is the answer to—or the mocking of—my question.

. ——— .

It was while I stood like a statue in my office among my potted houseplants and thought about Danny's coming to see me, about Danny's hoping to find a way to make me care about him, that I experienced "the bottom dropping out." It wasn't a sudden crash. It was more the way a sodden paper bag releases—dumps!—its load of groceries. Except in this case the groceries were the basic assumptions of my life and my profession. I stood there trying to catch one or two of them, to save something from falling. Everything was slipping out of my arms and through my fingers.

. ——— .

Eliza Peeler Scully
1850–1884
Too Soon
Called Away

· ——— ·

Much of what a therapist hears assaults what she believes. I've counseled husbands who beat their wives. Had I let my own experience of being abused by Jim Boscowen affect my response, I could not have functioned appropriately. I found I had the trick of empathy—I could enter even the brutal parts of their experience as if it were my own. I could even believe in their pain, and I persuaded myself that I had helped most of those husbands. I'd begun to think I was the ideal therapist for a wife beater. But I must have been hiding what I most deeply believed from myself, because on this afternoon of standing among my plants, without actually meaning to do so, I took stock of my life and my career. I could see my delusion so clearly: I'd given no real help to anyone. I had nothing to offer anyone. I was a fool.

· ——— ·

Less than a hundred years ago, this mountainside was a working farm. Thousands of years ago, after the glaciers melted away, there were no trees here at all. The landscape looked like the Arctic tundra.

· ——— ·

Pardon Scully
1868–1877
Beloved Boy

· ——— ·

Walking this way, I would be thought a child by anyone watching me. I take a few steps, look back to the birch at the corner of the graveyard, take a few more steps, and look back again to check my bearings. Already I'm accustomed to the circumstance of not being seen—what I look like doesn't matter anyway, and I have no desire to be lost within my first hours on the mountain. The grave-yard can be no more than a hundred yards or so from the home place. Already I've discerned how these Scullys gave their dead a plot of high ground. The land itself seems to wish to teach me how the family members wore their path into the hillside—its contours direct me when I set down my boots. The dead may be directing my footsteps, but I certainly don't trust them. They could be look-ing for company. If I lose sight of that tree, I could be lost in an instant and wander these woods for days; I could starve within fifty yards of my Jeep full of supplies. So I step through the shade and sunlight and keep looking back to the scrolling white column of the birch. It's not yet four o'clock, and perhaps I'm imagining it, but I feel a coolness rising from the ground. Benjamin and Eliza and Pardon and the others are sending up a cold shawl to drape over my shoulders.

· ——— ·

A tiny bird with a stubby, cocked tail breaks into such a long and beautiful song that I'm startled by it—and then amused. Raw talent is the phrase that occurs to me, but of course I don't say it aloud.

· ——— ·

There was no comfortable way to think about what I was doing. I'd been thinking about Danny and how powerfully aware I was that I was supposed to love the man I enjoyed sex with. I was thinking how miserable Danny was because of the same conven-tion. Then I was thinking of how so many of my clients were miserable because of one convention or another that trapped them or impelled them or made them feel they had failed. The first notion triggered by my little insight was that my job was to free people from the tyranny of conventions. That thought actually

forced from me a grim smile, because I had just seen myself as a
victim of such a convention. Why couldn't I free myself in the way
I'd thought I had helped free so many clients? But then this dark
thought came to me—that what my job actually was was to help
my clients move from the conventions that troubled them to conventions that gave them comfort. No matter that the comfort was
almost always temporary. If they needed a divorce but didn't feel
right about abandoning a marriage, I helped them consider the
new convention that being divorced is perfectly fine, it just takes
strength and resourcefulness. If they wanted to put a parent into
a nursing home, I helped them move away from the guilt convention to the convention that institutional care, in most cases, is
better for all concerned. If they wanted to throw a pot-smoking
kid out of the house, I helped them consider the convention of
tough love as something the kid might really need. No agent of
freedom or self-discovery or deeper truth, I was like a bartender
who says, "Oh, you're drinking all that bourbon, no wonder you
feel so terrible and behave so badly. Here, try scotch instead." I was
a delusion broker—I facilitated my clients' trading in one delusion
for another. Which skill no doubt accounted for the fact that the
woman standing there in my body, in her conventionally professional clothes, in her conventionally furnished office, among her
conventional potted plants, was—at that moment I could see it so
clearly—a profoundly deluded person.

· ——— ·

There's another bird whistling somewhere nearby. This one
I can't see, but it's not such a musical genius as the other.

· ——— ·

Looking back at my marking tree from maybe forty paces
away, I'm in a patch of sunlight where the softest breeze I've ever
felt rustles the leaves above me and coolly brushes my face. I let
myself stand here. I let go of everything in my mind except the
sight of that grayish-white tree trunk. I breathe the air that seems

almost too rich for my lungs. The smell is loamy, mushroomy. The slight current of air makes a sound in the woods like a motor running quietly in the distance. Tree limbs sway almost imperceptibly. The ferns at my knees flutter and stay, flutter and stay. I want to sit down in this mossy place, sit perfectly still and take it all in. When I look back through the tunnel of leaves and limbs to where I expect to see my guiding birch, it is not there. But of course that can't be. My heartbeat accelerates. I'm tempted to run in the direction of where I'm certain the tree is, but I have the good sense to stay still. I take a deep breath. Another.

. ———— .

A client told me of a fantasy she sometimes entertained. Everyone around her was setting her up, testing her to see if she could learn to be a real human being. Her parents and family and friends were all in on it, from even before she was born, everyone observing her carefully to see how she did with each little part of her test. Could she behave appropriately at a party? Handle a traffic jam? Write a check in a store? Kiss an old friend hello? Dress and undress in a locker room? Every little thing she did was a human skill she had to demonstrate. That's how I feel right now. The mountain—and everything here—is testing me to see if I belong.

. ———— .

In that single quiet hour of office time, my life's meaning disintegrated. I tried to retreat from hard thoughts about Danny to remembering Ben and how comfortable our married life had been. How dear Ben was in so many ways, bringing me the newspaper and my coffee just at the time I needed to wake up! That was what my mind tried to focus on and hold up to the light: how very dear Ben was. But whatever was at work on me was relentless. I couldn't even bring Ben's face clearly to mind. What I could bring back was the shock I felt one morning during our first week of marriage when I realized Ben was refusing my offer of sex. By then I had reconciled myself to the likelihood that sex with Ben wasn't ever going to be fulfilling, and so for me to make the offer was, in my view, a saintly act. And he was turning me down! No wonder he began bringing me coffee and the newspaper in the morning; less demanding to do that than to get into that bed with me where he belonged. I tried to argue with myself. I knew my insight about Ben was just a result of this disposition, this malicious thing that temporarily had hold of my spirit, even though somewhere in my mind such thoughts had probably been dimly present. But now the only thought that would come to me was that my deceased husband was a sexual wimp and a spiritual coward.

. ——— .

I force myself to twist around and look as far in the opposite direction as I can without moving my feet. Then I slowly turn back to where I expect to see the birch. "You're back!" I shout and immediately feel like a lummox, a bumbling human lummox who doesn't belong in the woods. I start to stride back to the tree, from which of course it is merely a distance of a few more steps to my Jeep. But something has snagged in my mind. I've seen something. As I was turning back around, my eyes took in some detail my mind is holding now like a secret it is willing to tell.

. ——— .

I'm getting a whiff of something pungent. Unwashed human being is what I'd ordinarily think it was—Fragrance of Funky Person—but I suspect it's a plant I've brushed up against. Skunk currant—didn't I read in the field guide about something up here called skunk currant? or wet dog trillium?

. ——— .

So I came to think about Peter Firkens, whom I had loved—or all these years believed myself when I was seven years old to have loved. In one of the first talks Danny and I had, I told him about my infatuation with Peter, who was our neighborhood paperboy. Telling Danny was the first time I'd put it into words. That was also when I became aware of how I had been sheltering that particular memory from others—as well as from myself, or from my adult mind. I've had the experience of suddenly catching a whiff of fragrance that takes me far back to something I adored as a child— cotton candy at the fair, wild strawberries in a field, a Christmas candle, or a dog's paw in the yard on a summer day. The scent will take me back so powerfully that what I feel is nearly unbearable. It's as if I've recovered something valued and lost, but now that I've found it again, I'm forced to accept just how permanently lost it is. So the very act of revisiting that beloved part of my childhood requires me to give it up. Instinctively, I had protected what I felt about Peter Firkens—I had avoided thinking about him too much or too intensely. I knew it was silly; you don't really possess the experience or the emotions you went through as a child. But it felt like a treasure I had packed away and held onto, the way, as a little girl, I sat on our front porch in Middlebury on summer afternoons and watched Peter walking down Waybury Street with his *Addison Independent* bag strapped around his shoulder—the way that sight of him made my whole body start humming, so that I could feel it even down in my butt and my thighs. Oh, it was a good thing!, such a very good thing, and it had come to be—whether real or not—something cherished that I possessed. I understood that taking it out and examining it would most likely make it disappear. Telling Danny about it, I had felt as if I had almost lost it, as if I'd better not revisit it or it would be taken from me. But alone in my office that afternoon, I was desperate to locate an experience of definite romantic love, something valuable and true. So that's what I did. I sat down and examined my childhood feelings about Peter Firkens.

· ——— ·

What I saw a moment ago, when I turned and swept my eyes through the green aisles of leaves and light, was a section of stone fence. Turning again, I see it maybe thirty yards downhill from where I stand. What else could it be but the old boundary of the home place?

· —— ·

When he wasn't wearing his baseball cap, Peter Firkens's straight brown hair angled down across his forehead so thickly I thought his hair must be three or four times as heavy as mine. He wore blue jeans and Converse sneakers, and he was slightly pigeon-toed—as, my father explained to my mother and me, most athletes are. In the fall, winter, and spring, he wore plaid flannel shirts—he had a couple of them, a mostly red one and a mostly-green one, and these were the shirts he favored. I paid attention to that—I even imagined there would come a time when I could say something like, "that red plaid shirt of yours, you know, your favorite one," and Peter would be so impressed that he would immediately start treating me like a big girl. The special thing about him was that he kept his shirt neatly tucked in. I had noticed that boys my age and older boys, too, on up into high school, tucked their shirts in any old way and didn't usually notice when their shirts came untucked. Peter's shirts were always arranged to be smooth in front and for the line of buttons to meet his belt buckle and the fly of his pants. He was somewhat soldierlike in his bearing, too, and I was certain I was the only person in the world who knew he took such trouble with his appearance. I was certain that I loved him.

· —— ·

To reach that little stretch of stone fence in the distance, I am going to have to give up the birch tree as my marker. While looking for a tree or bush to mark my new place, my eyes suddenly pick up an orange-capped bird, whose song I have heard for some minutes now. This tiny creature has been directly in front of me, on a branch at eye level, not ten feet away. *Haven't you been listening to me?* it scolds. *I'm sorry, pal*, I say. Since I am addressing another living creature, it feels less strange to speak aloud. A kinglet is what I think the field guide calls this one—I've had a conversation with the little king. And that's what I'm thinking when I begin bush-whacking my way down toward the stone fence. Saint Francis talked to the birds. Good enough for Saint F. Good enough for Claire McC.

· ——— ·

But I didn't love Peter Firkens. While I sat there thinking, it became starkly clear to me that what had moved me in my child-hood was a lot more science than it was romance. I was pas-sionately *interested* in Peter. And I was thwarted in my interest be-cause even though I studied him, I never found out much about him—which probably explains why I could sustain all these years of believing that I loved him. My interest in Peter Firkens was never satisfied, as it most certainly was with Jim and Ben and Danny. Until those moments in my office, I hadn't known the dif-ference between love and curiosity. I knew then that I had had no acquaintance with love, that I'd never grown beyond being drawn to males out of an urgent, childish wonder. It had been that way with Peter, Jim, Ben, and Danny: a driving curiosity, as if I had to know that person, as if I had to *be* that person. Now that I saw it so clearly, it seemed a dirty trick that my curiosity hadn't led to what I imagined love to be—tenderness, affection, desire, companion-ship, intense and abiding care. For my whole life I had been on the wrong track!

· ——— ·

When I reach the new section of stone wall, I look back up the wooded hillside to see if I'll be able to find my way back to my Jeep. What I see from where I stand is my Jeep. How I managed to execute such a maneuver, I don't know. I am the Columbus of Addison County, Vermont. I have discovered the configuration of landscape my father and I walked over almost twenty years ago. I'm exactly where I'm supposed to be. I got here by not knowing where I was going.

. ——— .

Maybe I had tricked myself into this revelation that I had never experienced love, that I had had no love in my life. I sat with my thoughts. It seemed entirely possible that the whole human species, from the time it crawled up out of the sea, had driven itself with exactly this delusion, mistaking curiosity for love. Also possible was that I had just intellectualized myself into a state of false wisdom. In either case, the realization ought to follow that, well, after all, I had known love in such and such a moment and with such and such a person. I sat still, waiting. No rescuing memory came to me. Most disturbing of all was remembering my parents—how my mother must have programmed herself to give me all that attention and how my father, who was distant anyway, felt he had to retreat even further after I married Jim. The longer I sat, the deeper my spirit plummeted, the whole system of my being descending to just breath and heartbeat.

. ——— .

A face among the leaves?

. ——— .

Just as I have remembered it, though it is almost invisible, the old dairy squats into this piece of land. Vegetation has grown up over and around it. There's no evidence that a human has set a foot here since those years ago when my father and I pushed open this door. When I push it now, at first it won't give. Then it does. The cool air washes against me. This dank cellary place has mightily exhaled. I sit down on the mossy ground at the entrance. The smell of the earth inside wafts out to me, and I can hear a mild current of wind overhead sifting through the trees. I don't know why I'm crying. For my father? For my father who cared for me before he drifted away.

· —— ·

That's how Danny found me, sitting among my houseplants, hardly breathing. I didn't want to come back. That afternoon my office blazed sunlight, but what I wanted was down at the bottom edge of breath and heartbeat, just one layer further down.

· —— ·

If you sit and stare into the leaves, you can imagine any number of forms. Shadows, green light, leaves, a face, a darkness that takes on this shape and that, and always movement—even in the stillest moment, a leaf twitches, a twig brushes a branch, something stirs or falls. Thousands of small noises every second. No such thing as silence.

· —— ·

With only a few hours of daylight left, I don't want to take up the project of trailblazing in order to move the Jeep closer. Now that I've found my place—my farm—I don't want to risk being lost again or stuck. Without entering the old dairy, I make my way back to the Jeep—slowly, but directly this time—and begin puttering among the packs and crates in the back. First I set up my small tent beside the Jeep. Then I set up my lantern and portable stove on the tailgate. This evening's menu at Cobb Hill Farm is bottled water, heated freeze-dried black bean soup, crackers, cheese, and mixed dried fruits. I am so hungry I have to force myself to eat slowly. I save my trash to be buried tomorrow, I dry-clean my dishes, I put everything away, and I close up the back of the Jeep. By the time the last of the daylight has drained from the sky, I am deeply snuggled into my sleeping bag, spinning my way into sleep, floating down through layers and layers of leaves, vines, and moss-covered tree limbs, a slow downward spiral into kaleidoscopic patterns of vegetation.

. ——— .

In the darkness a steady rattling surrounds me. I finally understand it to be rain pelting my tent, waking me from a deep sleep. I'm lucky there's no wind, because I took little trouble setting up my pegs and cords. I snake a hand out of my sleeping bag to feel the ground beside me. It's dry enough. It's too dark to see my watch, but I suspect it's not so long before daylight. I try to will myself back to sleep. All around me the tent walls make a low, percussive humming.

. ——— .

The only person with whom I ever really discussed suicide was Jim Boscowen. Which perhaps explains why I had that weird desire to talk with him before I left Bennington. But our old discussion was crazy, inane, pointless—one of a long series of talks Jim and I had after we were married in which he tried to bully me into respecting him and I tried to demonstrate to him how hopelessly pedestrian he was in his thinking. Jim's position was the standard one, that suicide is cowardice, surrender, a meanness to family and friends, and so on and so on. My position was that there are situations when suicide is appropriate. At the time I was just arguing. I was in graduate school, where it felt strange that my classmates and I shied away from talking about suicide outside the classroom even though it was something we were studying. Inside the classroom, discussion of suicide was limited to the practical matters of how to talk about it with clients, what to do to prevent it, and so forth. The gospel then, as it still is, was that any expression of interest in suicide was a danger signal—whoever spoke of it might do it—and so nobody spoke of it. As students, if we spoke of suicide outside the acceptable boundaries, we could be pulled out of our program and placed involuntarily on leave of absence "until the issue was resolved." We could lose the chance ever to become licensed practitioners, or even, for that matter, to graduate. So we didn't bring it up for casual discussion among ourselves. At home, however, I brought the topic up with Jim a lot. Jim and I both liked arguing about it. For us it was a hot topic.

. ——— .

The rain goes on well after daylight, which is slow in coming. I stay in the tent in my sleeping bag, awake but not eager to get up as long as it keeps raining. I let my mind drift. There was a time when I claimed to like rain. Before we were married, I once made Jim take a walk with me in a thunderstorm—no umbrellas, no rain slickers. I took off my shoes and sloshed through puddles and the muddy grass. Jim walked with his head down. He made it clear he was willing to do this idiotic thing for me, but he hated every minute of it. Now I suppose he's the one who's out there in the rain, running his shopping cart up and down the streets look-ing for bottles. And I'm the one who hates the rain. Even when I'm indoors I hate it. Or I don't hate it, but I resent it for steal-ing my energy. I don't feel like doing anything when it rains. This morning, when my bladder finally gets the best of me and the rain seems to be letting up a bit, I crawl out of the tent, stand up straight, stretch, and find myself staring down at a huge toad. The warty thing looks bored and judgmental, as if it's been wait-ing out here for me all morning. *Out of my way, Old Ugly*, I tell it. *I've got significant business to take care of.* Its throat pulses. When I return from my errand, the creature has disappeared.

. ——— .

I wish I had the nerve to enter the dairy without my flash-light, but I don't. Still outside, I switch it on, shine the light over the floor, then step inside, stand still, and shine it all around the walls, shelves, ceiling, corners, everywhere. It is like having broken through to the interior of a stone. The smell is as I remembered it—garden dirt, manure, worms, rain.

. ——— .

Danny was in me, and we had been holding at a certain level for a while. I was sweating and crazy with it. "Tell you something, Claire . . . ," Danny whispered. During sex, he and I almost never said anything. He was breathing hard and rocking me at such a pace, all I could manage was, "hunnnh?" and he said, ". . . just one true thing," and I said, "hunhhh?" and he rasped out, ". . . my cock in your cunt!" His words jolted down through my body, and I came so hard I thought I'd hurt myself. When it was over, I couldn't do anything but cry and tell Danny—who was concerned but also a little bemused—to get dressed and go, to leave me alone, I'd be all right after a while.

. ——— .

I tour the interior. Over every surface of the inside of the dairy, I shine the flashlight. I take time to examine it carefully. There are shelves on which are some crocks, and inside these crocks are long-ago rotted away liquids, milk or brandy or I can't say what. There's no scent in them stronger than the one marly scent of the place. There are bins where apples and potatoes must have been stored, and these, too, hold some dusty putrescence. The ceiling is clear of bats. I do not see a single spider or web. In corners where I expect to find nests of field mice, I don't. Nor is there evidence of flies, bees, ants, earwigs, or any sort of insect life. I don't know why living creatures seem to have eschewed this place, but I take it as a sign of good luck—it's a room prepared especially for me and awaiting my arrival.

When I'm satisfied I've seen it all, I close the door and walk to the middle of the open space. Standing there, I snap off the flashlight and hold still. I stay still a long time. It is a stone vault. Only the slightest line of gray light marks the bottom edge of the door. There are no sounds. My heartbeat and my breathing are all I hear, my body's incessant life. I take four steps to the door, open it, and walk, squinting, outside and over to a patch of sunlight on shimmering leafy fans. I sit down, blinking, assaulted by warmth, brightness, the smell of crushed ferns.

. ——— .

Carrying my packs and boxes the quarter mile from the Jeep to the dairy will take two or three full days, so I choose to scout out a trail to drive the Jeep in closer. But the project is not as difficult as I thought it would be. Twenty-five yards back down the logging road from where I stopped the Jeep, I find the contours of an old roadbed curving off the trail down into the home place. With the land nudging me this way and then that way, I walk the timeworn passage down almost to the dairy entranceway. Saplings and patches of something like sumac have grown up, but they are nothing the Jeep can't simply push down and run over. With a flick of the key I've got the Jeep running; I back up the necessary distance and then maneuver my machine down a roadbed formed by horses and wagons and buggies. It's idiotic, I know, but I'm proud of myself. It isn't even noontime yet, and I've accomplished three days' work.

· —— ·

A family of ravens must be nesting not far from here—three of them, I think, though there could be more. Again and again, they fly to my big spruce to heckle me or to announce my presence to the forest. *Old news*, I tell them. *I'm old news by now, you guys.* This is perhaps the longest period of time I've ever gone without speaking to another human being.

· —— ·

The water from the spring at Cobb Hill Farm is sumptuous and shockingly cold. It seems wasteful to let it trickle away down the mountain. The capitalist in me envisions plastic bottles labeled "Cobb Hill Green Mountain Springwater" selling in most grocery stores at ninety-five cents a quart. My Grandfather Thompson would be proud of me.

· —— ·

As if it were my front porch, I'm sitting out in front of the dairy in the folding chair I bought from Orvis. It's late afternoon, and I'm watching the light at the edge of a clump of birches. My eyes make out a bearded face there to the left of the birches. Then I can distinguish the man's body, crouched, monkeylike. Without shifting my eyes, I stand up and step slowly toward him, my heart clattering. He holds still. In two more steps, he dissolves into shadows. I haven't taken my eyes from him. I step forward. He's there. Then he isn't. I blink and keep moving. I walk directly through the place where he stood. When I step through the space his body occupied, my body registers a buzz of energy—also there then gone in an instant.

· ——— ·

Mornings, my mother sent me off to school and sent my father off to work; afternoons, she received us back home, first me and then him. Once, when I was around thirteen, in a surge of politeness I asked her how she spent her time when my father and I were not around. She snorted and said, "Oh, you'd be surprised." It was one of the few times I ever saw her look mischievous.

· ——— ·

Again tonight I set up my tent immediately beside the Jeep. Tomorrow I'll spend the day cleaning the dairy. As I'm settling down into my sleeping bag, for some strange reason I ask myself if I'm lonely. *Ha!* rudely bursts out before I have a chance to think. I have missed no one, and so the question obviously comes out of the stupid convention I've carried here with me, that anyone spending time alone must be lonely. But I can't seem to drop it. I do have this ache that I have always in the past named loneliness. And it is the same ache, I tell myself. But if anything, I've been less aware of it since I left Rutland yesterday. I was lonely when I was seeing clients and colleagues and friends all day long. So the correct answer is, no more than usual. No, the correct answer is, I'm a lot less lonely now that I'm out here by myself.

· ——— ·

If there were a man around here, he would have to be abnormal.

Am I abnormal?

Yes. The answer to that question is yes.

So there could be a man out here who is like me?

Not likely.

Still, it's possible, isn't it?—I'm here; and so couldn't there be somebody else here for similar reasons?

In my dreams.

"What can be dreamed can actually be." Didn't somebody once say something like that?

No.

Still, what can it hurt, just admitting the possibility of a man who's out here for the same reason I am?

It hurts my sense of reality, that's what it hurts!

So?

So it's losing touch with the real world.

The real world is my office, my clients, Danny Marlow coming to see me once a week. The real world is me getting sick of my life. Why, exactly, did I come out here if not to lose touch with the real world?

A man could want the same thing.

An educated man?

I guess he would have to be educated. Yes, that seems essential.

· ——— ·

In the early morning I locate a place thirty paces away and dig a latrine. At first the ravens serenade me. Then they hush and sit high up in the trees. When I have dug it to my satisfaction, I use it. *Watch this*, I tell my witnesses as I squat. *You guys need some binoculars!* I shout up to them.

· ——— ·

Black flies are evidence not only that there is a god but that god is bitter and treacherous.

· ——— ·

I set the lantern going and carry it inside, along with the broom I brought from home just for this purpose. Anything I can pick up—the crocks, a couple of ancient wooden crates, a head-sized stone they must have used for a doorstop—I carry out and set in the sunlight. By my calculations, the human creature can, without undue strain, execute approximately twenty-five broom strokes per minute. By my calculations—because the mind tends to occupy itself while the body moves through repetitive tasks—I execute approximately six thousand broom strokes in the interior of the dairy. I sweep the floor, the ceiling, the walls, the shelves, any sweepable surface. The dirt my broom collects probably weighs no more than a couple of pounds. Nevertheless, this work is necessary. *Claire takes possession of her new home,* I announce to the afternoon sunlight when I step outside at the conclusion of my sweeping. I make a grand gesture with my broom. *Claire shall sleep in her new home tonight,* I say to my Jeep and my tent.

· ——— ·

Corned beef hash—heated
Canned beets—heated
Cobb Hill Green Mountain Springwater—cold

· ——— ·

As best he could, my father disguised his disdain for Jim Boscowen. After Jim and I married, my father just faded away from me. He had dinner with us a few evenings, but I could tell he hated it, and then he began having less and less to do with us. I kept wanting to "recover" him, to pull his attention back to me. I was admitted to graduate school and started doing very well. I knew he liked for me to achieve academically, even if I had to do it as a married student. Then he died. And I felt as if I had never gotten enough of him. Jim's abuse began not so long afterward. He said things to me I knew he never would have said if my father had still been alive. He screamed at me. He even lifted his hand as if to slap me. If I hadn't been still grieving for my father, I'd never have let him treat me that way. But Jim's hateful behavior seemed to go with my father's having left me alone in the world. By merely being alive, my father had protected me, and so his death made me vulnerable. There wasn't any sense to the way I felt, but for a while I think I was more angry at my father than at Jim. I understand the deaths of parents to be natural events in the course of a lifetime; nevertheless, I have had to struggle against what the deaths of my mother and father have done to me.

· ——— ·

With the door to the dairy still open to let in the evening's last light, I set up my cot and lay my sleeping bag on it. Then I light my lantern. I close the door and with my foot push the head-sized boulder against it. There is a depression in the stone doorstep into which the boulder fits exactly. This groove is so shallow I haven't even noticed it until now, but it would take a mighty push against the door from the outside to unseat that boulder. To make a lock, someone carved the groove to fit the stone. Someone conceived of being in here with this door locked against something or somebody outside—there's a thought to take to bed with me! I'm so tired, though, it doesn't matter. I'm certain I'll sleep soundly. In here I feel safe enough now to undress down to my underpants and a T-shirt. Before I shut off the lantern, I set my flashlight on the floor in easy reach. Then I lie back in the blackest dark I've ever known.

· ——— ·

Collect springwater for a bath.
Move everything from the Jeep into my cave.
Consider possible garden site.

· ——— ·

I'm awake and seeing nothing. Then I'm seeing the little bar of grayness that is the bottom edge of the door. In my cave, sunup apparently registers as a slight graying of the blackness. This is the first morning I've felt no urgency about my plans. I came to this place because here nothing will hurry or distract me. Nevertheless, I'm here with a certain vagueness. Nothing is definite yet. I hope to recognize the right time when it arrives. And when the right time arrives, I'm assuming I'll know the right method. Most likely I'll spend the summer and early fall instructing myself as I need to. Most likely I'll not wish to attempt to survive a winter up here. Most likely I'll want to use the supply of Halcion tablets I brought with me. But I am open to possibility. My only requirement is that I have ample opportunity to feel and to think. In the moment I choose to leave this world, I want to be as present in it as I have ever been.

· ——— ·

Opening the door, I witness a swirling of morning light and vapor that for an instant becomes the person I hallucinated yesterday. Stark naked, he strides away from my grounds, having examined my Jeep, having sat in my folding chair, and having spat on my ferns and crabgrass. *Make yourself at home*, I tell him before his backside dissolves in the green shadows. My spoken words linger in the bright air.

· ——— ·

I had no wish to cause Danny pain. I could have explained myself to him in terms of what the textbooks say about fear of intimacy. Maybe that would have made things easier for him. But I didn't want to insult him. And I would have been lying anyway, because finally those books didn't apply to the way I felt—dirty and glorious all at once. I didn't really even want an explanation for why he touched off in me what he did. But if I hadn't wanted him the way I did, I think I might have liked him very much.

· ——— ·

A bath is a problem. The springwater is just too cold to use directly from the spring. I have two one-gallon buckets. So I collect the two bucketfuls, leave them sitting in the sunlight, and go poking about. Some of the foundation of the Scullys' house remains. There are layers of deeply rotted wood, shards of glass and metal, nothing recognizable or useful. There's even a smell of rot that I perceive now as being constantly in the air but thickest here over the ruins of the house. The place repels me. I don't really want to find anything useful or informative. I walk away from the ruins and over to my chair and my buckets of water. It is pleasant enough to sit in the morning sunlight. After a while I enter time itself—like a deep, smooth river, it carries me along. I am warm in the light. The leaves flutter. At the edge of my vision, my mirage of a man is out there moving among the trees. When the sun warms me sufficiently, I stand up, luxuriously remove my clothes, stretch in the light, take up my sponge and soap, and begin bathing.

. ——— .

The ravens make their comments.

. ——— .

A major success! Two maples that must have marked the front entrance to the Scullys' yard are exactly the right distance apart for my hammock. I nail the metal pieces into each tree, insert the wooden rods into their sleeves at the head and foot of the hammock, and stretch the cloth-and-rope apparatus from one hook to the other. Perfect! When I sit in it, my butt is a couple of feet off the ground. I lie down and try to relax, but I am too exhilarated. I have to get up and walk around and inspect it. The only other hammock I have had was set up by my father on my tenth birthday. Now, when I am almost forty, I am discovering these new dimensions to my personality—*Claire the practical, Claire the handywoman!* I set my mind to other projects for the summer. The most obvious, of course, is a garden.

. ——— .

In the late afternoon it gradually becomes cloudy. Then comes a small rain that evidently means to increase throughout the afternoon and evening. I don't particularly want to be in my cave, but I also don't want to sit in my Jeep or set up my tent. The compromise is a makeshift porch roof outside the dairy door that I quickly improvise by draping my tent this way and that over its propped-up poles. Claire the handywoman does a lousy job. No sooner do I sit down in my chair than the wind comes up and the porch comes down—on top of me. I laugh as I pull the whole wet mess into the dairy, but in here, in the dark, it's not funny anymore.

· ——— ·

The dairy is a chamber of suspension. It waits. When I come inside it, the dairy says *Shhhh!* The dairy says *Be quiet!* My pulse slows.

· ——— ·

Claire the potato.

· ——— ·

Tonight I can't bring myself to close the door. Why should I? Even the mosquitoes won't come in. If my man of the forest wants to come in, well all right. Tonight I could use the company. I don't mind the sound of the rain out there, but for some reason it makes me feel just so forlorn.

· ——— ·

I don't know how there could be any light coming in here from outside with such a rain falling, but there is, the thinnest gray glimmer. I've lain here with my eyes open, watching it so long it's become my friend. Finally, I get up and locate one of the containers of sleeping medication. I put a tablet in my mouth and swallow. Then I slip back beneath my covers. Now, with the light coming, reaching my cot, brushing over me, I know I can sleep.

· ——— ·

My mother's hand on my forehead. I love her cool hand right there where I am too hot. *Leave your hand there, please,* I want to tell her, but she goes away before I can speak. Then she is back with my father, their worried faces staring down at me. *Put your hand back on my forehead, and I'll be all right,* I want to tell my mother, but I'm not able to utter the necessary sounds.

· ——— ·

"What's that plate number?" I hear shouted as if through a tunnel from some distance away. This is a man's voice that wakes me. In a moment, another man's voice, still farther away, sounds out the numbers of my Jeep's license plate. I lie still and listen to what seem to be only two voices conversing. My cave is cool and dim. Through the open doorway, I can see that it has stopped raining and that it's bright outside; my doorway gives me a rectangle of lighted greenness. Apparently, I've slept deeply into the day. It can be only a minute or two before these men discover the dairy entrance. The thought occurs to me that I can get up, close the door, and slide the locking boulder into place. I can delay them that much. But I don't. Something rises in me. I want to see whoever's out there. I want to see their faces. I get up and dress quickly. I even have the urge to find clean clothes, to comb my hair. But of course I don't. I walk outside, and they are standing there as if they've been waiting for me, green uniformed young men. They wear badges and straps and holstered pistols. When I approach, they blink as if I've stepped out of another dimension. *I have!* briefly crosses my mind. "Yes?" I say, looking from one to the other, marveling at their intricate features, their elaborate uniforms, their tanned forearms, their laced boots, their rectangular name tags. "Yes, gentlemen?" I say again, stepping toward them.

"Are you Claire McClelland?" asks the one holding an open notebook, glancing up as if to compare the real me to a picture he's brought along. The other, the mustached one, looks down, away from me. It hurts my feelings that that second one won't look at me.

. ——— .

"I am," I say.

. ——— .

They are Officers O'Brien and Desautels from the U.S. Forest Service. They have to keep an eye out for people who grow marijuana, and they are looking into a report they received that someone might be camping in this part of the woods. They have also been on the alert for a missing person—myself.

My face burns with the shock of finding that someone has been aware of my presence here. I go back inside and fetch up my papers for them. I bring out the folder and show them my deed to the Cobb Hill Farm. "Am I doing anything illegal?" I ask. Officer O'Brien shrugs and says he supposes not, at least not so far as he knows. I ask them if they must report my whereabouts to the authorities. They look at each other and nod. They must, O'Brien says. I ask them if my whereabouts can remain a confidential matter. They look at each other and shrug.

"We can try to keep it out of the papers, ma'am, but something has to go into the public record," Officer Desautels tells me.

I ask them to do their best. I tell them that my privacy is very important to me. I turn back to the dairy. I'm about to carry my deed back inside, because I have the irrational notion it will be harmed by the open sunlight.

Officer O'Brien, the one with the notebook, speaks up. "Do you mind if we take a quick look inside there, ma'am?"

This stops me. I turn and look from one to the other of the two men. "Why do you want to do that?" I ask.

They give me their cowlike regard. "Just so we can be sure you're safe, ma'am. The reports said you might have been kidnapped. We wouldn't want there to be somebody hiding in there, forcing you to send us away."

"There's no one here but me," I say. "Do you have a search warrant?"

"No, ma'am."

"So I can say no?"

"Yes, ma'am. You can say no. But then we'll probably have to come back. Or the state police will."

Again they stare at me, and I at them. We are at a standoff, though of course I am no match for them. My only source of power is the document I hold that makes this land mine. Each of them is at least half again as large as I am. They're somewhat younger and a great deal stronger. They have uniforms and name tags and weapons. As I think about it, the circumstance nauseates me. "I don't want you going in there," I tell them in a voice so low it's nearly a whisper.

"Ma'am, if you're interested in guarding your privacy, it'd probably be easier just to let us have a quick look now," Officer Desautels says. "But it's up to you."

"Can't you just go away?" I hear myself saying.

"Yes, ma'am," Officer O'Brien says in a voice of supreme calmness. "But we'll have to come back. Or somebody will."

The man's tone tells me as clearly as if he had said it straight out, *We think you're crazy.* Then I see myself through the eyes of these two young men, a middle-aged woman whose hair hasn't been washed or brushed in several days, whose boots are unlaced, and whose shirt isn't tucked in or even completely buttoned. I see how they are looking at me. It is all I can do not to blurt out, "I took a bath yesterday! I have a Ph.D. in psychology! I'm one of the most respected professionals in Bennington, Vermont! I have a lover who could pick the two of you up and turn you upside down and shake all the change out of your pockets!" Instead, I step to one side and gesture with my hand toward the door of the dairy. I glower at the men, but I say nothing.

Bowing their heads, they step into my cave. I don't follow them in. I can't stand to see them in there. I stay where I am, a fury raging inside me.

After a minute or two, Officers O'Brien and Desautels duck under the doorway, step outside again, thank me, and bid me good-bye and to take care. I have nothing else to say to them. I watch their backs moving into the woods away from me. I hope my naked man of the forest ambushes them and slits their throats, avenging what they have done to me.

· ——— ·

I can't go in there. I pace. When the ravens come to caw at me, I look for something to throw at them.

· ——— ·

Even springwater won't cool me down. I gulp it, but I can't calm myself.

· ——— ·

There's a wind today. When I sit in my chair, willing myself to be still, every blade, limb, and leaf stirs around me. The trees sway and suffer. Fat clouds sail overhead. Sitting still, I'm cold, but I can't make myself go in there for my jacket. To keep from shivering, I get up and pace again.

· ——— ·

I notice that I have been carrying the folder with my deed in it, clutching it in one hand, then the other.

· ——— ·

My forest man runs this way and that through the trees, just far enough away so I can't see him clearly. He breaks sticks, throws stones, and kicks at the underbrush. He snarls "O'Brien" and "Desautels" and spits.

· ——— ·

In the late afternoon I know I have to go inside. I make myself sit down and prepare for what I may see. If they have disturbed anything— if they have even touched my cot!—I swear I will—

. —— .

Once, standing at my desk, naked, and glancing back at Danny, I saw him lying back on the floor with his head propped up on his hands and staring at me. I saw how his eyes took in the sight of my naked back. I covered myself as best I could and quickly lay back down beside him—but not out of shyness or the desire to be close. Only to take the sight of me away from him.

. —— .

Inside, I find they poked around just enough to discover my handgun. In Montpelier or Rutland, Officers O'Brien and Desautels will report that pistol to their superiors, who in turn will probably dispatch a team of "professionals" here to coax me down out of the mountain. I'm guessing I have about twenty-four hours before I will have to negotiate the terms of my life with strangers. Worse yet, I probably know at least one member of that team, the one that comes out of Rutland—a "suicide prevention specialist" who was a graduate school classmate of mine. Whatever crime it is that I have committed, this punishment is unusually hateful.

. —— .

"Everything tells you something." I am saying this to myself, this thing my father once said to me. It isn't a bad thing to be saying.

. —— .

This is a terrible place. I can't keep the lantern lit, can't sit or lie down on my cot, can't find a place even to stand comfortably. Finally, I set my chair as close to the open doorway as I can and try to sit facing the light that is slowly dimming over the deep green-ness outside. This is bearable.

· ——— ·

I am listening. I know to do this. In the hours that pass, I feel myself listening more and more intensely. Whatever this place can tell me, I am here to hear it. I am here to hear.

· ——— ·

It's still windy outside. I don't know the time. I'm frozen where I sit. But I can see out into the grayness as clearly as if it were daylight. The dark silhouette that is my forest man, with his head down, walks slowly toward my doorway. He comes so close I can almost smell his beasty stench on the slight current of wind wafting in through the door. Out there he sits down, too, on the ground just to the side so I can't see the whole of him. But I see enough to know that he sits two paces away with his arms crossed over his knees and his head bowed on his hands. It comes to me then that he is grieving for me! I don't know why this calms me, but it does. It's as if he has taken away the pain I have felt building for many months. All through my body, my muscles loosen. I straighten in my chair. Alert and intent now, I go on listening.

· ——— ·

I thought there might be an animal or a snake that I would need to shoot. The pistol was never to use on myself. The pills were what I had in mind to use.

· ——— ·

How do I know this? My father would not disapprove.

· ——— ·

My mother would.

. ——— .

The wind dies down. The sky clears. It lightens outside. The message is clear. It is a relief finally to accept what has become so evident. I have no one. There is no place for me in this world. If I had any doubts about this being a place for me, they have been removed by Officers O'Brien and Desautels. I stand up—after having not moved for several hours—and go to the pack where I have stored the sleeping medication. I take out the three small, plastic bottles and set them beside my chair. Then I pick up my full canteen and carry it with me back to the chair. I sit down again, with the canteen in my lap and the little bottles beside me where I can reach them. Outside, my poor forest man sobs into his crossed arms.

. ——— .

Am I here? *Completely.*
Do I want to be here? *No. Not anymore.*
I pick up the first bottle.

. ——— .

When my mother died, my father and I were sitting on either side of her bed. We were holding her hands. Earlier in the evening, while she was conscious, we had talked with her. I had washed her face and tried to brush her hair. My father and I had each in turn told her that we loved her. My father had known to tell her she was brave, which had made her smile at him. This was in the hospital in Boston. Our doctor had told us it wasn't likely she would last many more hours. They had removed the tube to her stomach and her IV and had taken her off all medications except the one for pain. The nursing staff told us to buzz if we needed anything, otherwise they would leave us alone. So it was just the three of us in the room. Deep into the night it became quiet as a satellite moving through space. For several hours my mother hadn't been conscious, though her breathing was slow and steady. Abruptly, my father released her hand, stood up, moved to the head of the bed, leaned down, and placed his hand on my mother's forehead. "All right, Helen," he murmured—at least that's what I think he said; his voice was very low, his head very close to hers. There was the slightest fluttering of her eyelids, her expression seemed to relax, then her breathing changed—slowed. Finally she took a breath that I thought would be the last one, and it was. My mother was there, then she wasn't there anymore. My father and I were looking at each other, not a long time but long enough for me to remember exactly how his face was. It was not the face of a man who'd lost the love of his life. It was the face of a man who had carried out an inspired performance. My father knew that I understood that. He knew that I appreciated it exactly for what it was.

. ——— .

Can't you help me with this? I find myself asking. Knowing how silly I am to speak like this to my made-up forest man, I'm smiling. *Please,* I say anyway.

. ——— .

Three tablets at a time. Plenty of water in the canteen.

. ——— .

Swallow.

. ——— .

Do it, Claire!

. ——— .

No?!

. ——— .

As if someone had tried to make me eat a green vegetable I didn't like, I'm gagging. My stupid, treacherous body just won't do it. What it apparently will do is shiver and sweat.

. ——— .

Doesn't matter if I hurt. If it hurts me just to be alive. Don't have a choice. Thought I did, but I don't.

. ——— .

Life sentence.

. ——— .

He comes in. On his own. I never thought he would. His grief for me distorts his face and makes him look even more beastlike. He can't speak—I know that. He can't touch me. Still, he is doing what he can, bringing his body and his stench right up to my chair. *I know you can't really do this*, I tell him. He struggles on my behalf. His face twists in his effort to speak to me. *It's not really necessary*, I say. He reaches toward my face with the most filthy, gnarled, and scarred hand.